About the Author

SL Harris lives in rural Missouri with her partner of many years. A physical therapist and long-time reader, her vision began to diminish and she lost access to her beloved books. After several surgeries, much of her vision was restored. She began reading again, discovered the world of lesbian fiction and began to write her own stories. *Laughter in the Wind* is her first novel.

Acknowledgments

I am eternally grateful to all the wonderful people at Bella Books for permitting my dream to become a reality.

Special thanks to Katherine V. Forrest, who patiently guided me through the editing process—I was truly honored to learn from you.

To my friends who encouraged me, thank you all. What an awesome team we are!

Ruth, thank you for believing in me. You complete me.

Finally, I thank God for this life I've been given.

CHAPTER ONE

At nine-thirty p.m. on Halloween night, a lone car eased through Springtown, down Pine Street, past the churches, the beauty shop and the small general store. The car windows, tinted beyond the legal limit, reflected the lights from the windows of the small homes that lined this center street of town. At the south edge of the sleepy town the car turned down a gravel road, heading west.

The Whitman house was dark as the car slowly idled past. Mrs. Whitman had died two years earlier and all the locals knew Mr. Whitman took his hearing aids out and went to bed at seven-thirty. One-half mile further down the road was Jim and Patsy Wilcox's house. Their grown children no longer lived at home and Jim and Patsy were in Rockford for dinner and a movie, so their house was dark except for a porch light. Surprisingly, the car did not slow or stop at their drive although it was the final residence on the road. It continued around the next curve in the road to a dilapidated old house, long deserted and beginning to bend with the weight of its age.

The car pulled up in front of the old house, its headlights briefly illuminating the sagging roof of the porch and the broken steps to the entrance. Moments later, the driver's door opened and a man with a flashlight stepped out. He walked to the left side of the drive and opened an old gate into the overgrown pasture beside the house. He returned to the car then cut the wheels sharply to the left to ease the car down a faintly visible path through the gate and along a grove of trees. The lane was high with weeds and grass which brushed against the bottom of the car and occasional low-hanging limbs overhung the car's path, screeching painfully along the sides and top and leaving long scratches in the paint. As the car proceeded, the headlight beams picked up a rickety fence, then the looming headstones of an old cemetery.

The driver pulled the car to a stop in front of the gate to the cemetery, which was hanging at an odd angle from only the top hinge. Three car doors opened and the occupants of the car emerged, walking forward into the overlapping twin shafts of light from the high beams the driver had left on when he stopped the car.

The driver, a tall, thin man, opened the cemetery gate cautiously, careful to keep it connected to its lone hinge. "I'll see if this is the right place," he told the others as he lifted his large flashlight and stepped closer to the headstones. He carefully inspected several of the markers, stopping finally at a rectangular, upright stone. He stooped closer to read an inscription that was faded by the elements.

"This is it," he said, as he rose to his full six feet, seven inches of height. "Bring the box and the shovels."

The passenger who climbed from the front seat was a petite woman, more than a foot shorter than the driver. She disappeared into the rear seat of the car and reappeared seconds later with a wooden box about a foot long and eighteen inches square. She cradled the box to her like a precious work of art and stepped gingerly through the tall grass toward the driver. Their companion, a slightly obese man of medium height, retrieved

Laughter in the Wind

SL Harris

Bella
BOOKS
2013

Bella Books, Inc.
P.O. Box 10543
Tallahassee, FL 32302

Printed in the United States of America on acid-free paper.

First Bella Books Edition 2013

Editor: Katherine V. Forrest
Cover Designed by: Linda Callaghan

ISBN: 978-1-59493-354-7

two shovels from the trunk of the car and was only a step or two behind the woman.

Without another word, the men began to dig directly in front of the stone over the old grave site. Their task was finished in less than thirty minutes. The box was buried three feet deep and only a mound of dirt patted down firmly with their shovels remained as evidence of their efforts.

"It's done," the woman said simply. "I pray Mother will forgive us."

They stood around the pile of dirt for a few seconds in silence, heads bowed, holding hands. Then they quickly brushed the dirt from their clothes, loaded the shovels into the trunk and stepped back into the car. The driver slowly backed the car along the narrow lane, following the same tracks he had made when he approached the cemetery. The headlights highlighted the open gate, still hanging lopsided from the single hinge.

* * *

For Rebecca Wilcox, Halloween morning started like most other Saturdays. When she walked into the kitchen for coffee and breakfast, in that order, her mother was sitting at the table, nose in a newspaper as usual.

"Morning," Rebecca muttered as she filled a bowl with cereal. "Dammit," she said under her breath as cereal spilled over the edge of the bowl onto the table and the floor.

"Rebecca, is that really necessary?" her mother's voice prodded gently.

Rebecca knew she didn't like her to curse but for some reason, this morning she didn't care. "Spilling the cereal or 'dammit?'" she replied smartly then was immediately remorseful. "Sorry, Mom. I guess neither is necessary. I just woke up in a mood."

The newspaper had dropped unceremoniously onto the table at her sassy remark and the quick spark in her mother's eyes did not go unnoticed. A long pause followed her apology and she watched her mother's face, waiting for the response she knew she deserved but hoping her mother would show her some mercy. Rebecca wasn't sure what to expect, as she seldom spoke back to her mother.

"Bec, what's wrong? I don't mean just now, although I wouldn't have expected to hear you get smart with me. You've been upset about something for weeks now and I don't like to see you in this turmoil. What's going on?"

As usual, her mother, always supportive of her daughters, didn't fail to quickly get to the heart of the matter. Rebecca sighed deeply, partly in relief and partly in frustration. She tried to come up with an answer as she swept up the spilled cereal. She poured milk into the bowl then sat down at the table, keeping her eyes carefully averted from her mother. "I don't know that anything is wrong, Mom. Maybe it's just me. Maybe I'm just turning into a grumpy adult." She smiled half-heartedly at her mother.

"Good try, Bec. But you can't avoid this…this whatever-it-is that's bothering you. Sooner or later, you're going to have to deal with it."

"I don't know what's bugging me. Maybe I just miss my friends. Sandy called and I'm going to Rockford with her tonight. Maybe I'll wake up tomorrow and be back to my old self." She tried to sound upbeat and positive but knew she failed when she saw the concern still evident in her mother's expression before she picked up her crumpled paper and shook it back into shape, returning to her reading without another word.

Off the hook for the moment.

This was Rebecca's first Halloween since graduating high school and she was looking forward to going out with her friends, eating pizza and cruising Rockford. She really wasn't in the mood for cruising, but pizza and hanging out with her friends sounded good. She hoped the evening would ease her feelings of discontent. She didn't recognize the sullen person she had become and wished she could be the happy, confident Rebecca again.

* * *

When Sandy pulled up in her driveway at five, Rebecca was waiting at the door. On the thirty-minute drive to Rockford, she listened quietly as Sandy filled her in on Darwin, her on-again, off-again boyfriend. Currently off-again, she wasn't surprised to learn. Rebecca had warned Sandy about him before she ever started dating him, but the fact that he seemed to have a different girlfriend every other week hadn't deterred her. Sandy was as headstrong as Rebecca and no one could tell her that she wouldn't be the one Darwin would finally stick with.

As they neared the edge of town, Rebecca's patience finally ran out. "Sandy, you've always known he's a jerk. Just move on and forget his two-timing ass."

Sandy looked over in surprise at her usually quiet, calm friend who was staring straight ahead, a look of disgust on her face. "Damn, what's gotten into you, Bec? You know, it's not that easy to just forget about someone you really care about."

Rebecca could hear the pout in her voice and knew Sandy relied on her to be supportive, not to tell her she was wrong even if it was the truth. "Look, Sandy. I'm sorry. You're right. It's gotta be hard to just let go. But at some point you're gonna have to ask yourself if he's worth all this shit. You get to be all screwed up over him and he gets to chase after any girl he wants, knowing you'll be there to catch him if he falls. I guess I just don't see what's in it for you."

"You'll understand the first time you fall in love, Bec." Sandy still sounded a little put-out but Rebecca wasn't in the mood to lie to her and tell her she was right, so she just sat quietly for the few blocks remaining to the pizza place.

Connie and Pam had saved them seats and Rebecca was relieved to see her friends. She quickly realized her relief was premature when the conversation became a competition between her three friends, each trying to one-up the others with how her boyfriend had wronged her. Rebecca sat quietly in the corner thinking about how much more peaceful life seemed to be from her own perspective. Maybe she would be just like her friends if she had a boyfriend. After listening to her friends for a while though, she wasn't so sure that it would be worth it. Feeling discontented sure beat all this shit, she thought as she smiled to herself.

After filling up on pizza and downing several glasses of cherry Coke, she climbed into the back seat of Pam's mother's Escape and they cruised the streets of Rockford. She sat quietly looking out the window as Sandy moved to the middle of the seat to lean forward and look out the windshield with Pam and Connie. They saw few people they recognized and no one they knew well enough that they would stop and talk. Nevertheless, they made the circuit between downtown and McDonald's a hundred times in Rebecca's estimation, with Pam, Connie and Sandy honking and waving at every cute guy they saw along the way. Rebecca could see in her mind a picture of the four of them in the car and wondered why she looked so out of place.

What's wrong with me? Or are they the ones that are crazy?

Sandy apparently noticed she had remained withdrawn from them all evening and on the way home attempted to discover what was wrong. Rebecca wasn't sure what was wrong or how to even begin to explain so she made an excuse about being up late all week cramming for a test in her college algebra class. The excuse must have rung true because Sandy didn't press her further.

When Sandy dropped her off at her house it was ten-thirty, still early for a Saturday night. Rebecca suspected Sandy would meet Connie and Pam again in Freedom, the next town south of Springtown where they had all attended high school together and where the other three lived. She didn't mind that she hadn't been invited along for more fun cruising.

Her parents were already asleep and the house was dark and quiet. She stepped quietly down the hall and to her room where she sprawled across her bed and stared out the window. Her mind turned in circles like a runaway Ferris wheel and she wasn't sure how to get it to stop. At her high school graduation, everyone had said that the world awaited the graduates, a world full of possibilities. Why did it feel now like the world around her had grown smaller? It was as if she had missed something, like a door to part of her life had closed behind her but another door hadn't opened in its place, or maybe she just hadn't been looking when it did. She imagined herself in different scenarios: in a dorm room at a four-year college, standing beside the perfect man, or as an accomplished professional in one career or another. Nothing seemed right.

Out of the corner of her eye she saw two small lights, like headlights, out her bedroom window. She guessed they were probably a mile away but was surprised when she couldn't place where they would be coming from. She had stared out that window thousands of times over the years and couldn't remember ever seeing lights there before.

Oh well, maybe I'm seeing things. Guess I really am crazy.

She gave up thinking about it all and went to bed. Her head hit the pillow about the same time as the strangers' car hit the blacktop.

CHAPTER TWO

A week later, Halloween weekend had been put out of her mind. Rebecca awoke with a single thought: fishing. She realized as she dressed for the cool outdoors how much she loved Saturday mornings. It was the only day of the week she felt totally free. No classes, no work and no family dinners meant no responsibilities and no watching the time. On this Saturday, the first weekend of November, she planned to hike across a couple of pastures to fish in her uncle's catfish pond. It would have been quicker to drive but she enjoyed walking through the fields, seeing the changes the seasons brought to the plants and animals around her. She found it relaxing after being cooped up in a brick school building most of the week.

"Mom, I'm walking over to Uncle Jim's catfish pond," she yelled into the house as she headed for the garage to gather her pole and tackle box.

"Did you take a round bale out for the cows like your father asked?" her mother asked as she emerged around the corner of the garage.

"No, but I'm going now." Rebecca put her tackle box back on the shelf and retraced her steps to the house. She donned a heavier jacket with a hood and a pair of lined leather gloves. Her rubber boots were already on so all that was left was getting the tractor key from the key rack by the door. "I'll be back in a few," she told her mother as she passed her on her way to the tractor.

She really didn't mind feeding the cows and when her parents had suggested she take on more chores when she graduated from high school, she jumped at the chance for this job over something like housework. Some of it she tolerated but endlessly dusting her mother's knickknacks she hated with a passion.

She fired up the tractor then maneuvered it over to the rows of round bales she and her father had brought in from the hayfield the previous June. Backing up to the nearest bale, she drove the spike on the back of the tractor into the center of the bale then used the hydraulic lift to pick up the bale. Climbing down from the tractor, she opened the gate to the pasture.

"Come on, Daisy, back up." She slapped the bony hip of the black cow remaining steadfastly in the center of the opening to the pasture. Daisy was one of her favorites but was also one of the most stubborn cows in their herd. Finally satisfied they were far enough back, she jogged back to the tractor, climbed up and drove quickly through the gate. She continued out into the field without shutting the gate, knowing the cows would follow the hay and the tractor.

When she reached the slope where she would unroll the hay, she climbed down again, removed the green netting from the hay then pushed the cows out of her way to get back to the side of the tractor so she could climb back onto it. She lowered the bale to the ground then eased the tractor forward, sliding the bale off the spike. She pulled the tractor around to the uphill side of the bale, honked a few times to move the cows out of her way and used the loader on the front of the tractor to roll the bale down the slope. The bale unrolled as it slowly tumbled down the hill and the cows quickly stepped up and began eating hay along the length of the yellow path it left.

Rebecca stood on the tractor and counted the cows and their calves. "All present and accounted for," she said aloud.

She turned the tractor around and drove it out of the field. After parking it beside the rows of bales, she shut and latched the gate. "Now it's time to fish," she said.

Her mother heard her come into the house to change jackets and followed her back outside afterward. "Be back by five," she said, shaking her head as she watched Rebecca gather worms from her worm bed then pick up a smelly bag of chicken livers and toss it in a bucket to take along.

"Yes Mom," Rebecca groaned. Actually she had no other plans for the day and would probably be home well before then, but she felt like she should protest a little just to remind her mother she wasn't a kid anymore. She would be nineteen in four months and she had been a college student for the past three months. She headed out across the yard to the pasture fence, her mind already moving ahead to the upcoming battle between her and the fish, or at least to a few hours lazing on the pond bank letting the fish steal her bait.

It was a cool morning, only thirty-eight degrees, but it was supposed to hit sixty degrees by two o'clock. Fishing today probably wouldn't be good but Rebecca didn't care. It wasn't really about catching fish. Something about sitting on the bank of a pond or river, watching the water move and listening to it lap gently onto the bank, was as pleasurable to her as the ballet she had attended the previous year with the High School Honor Society. She didn't want to miss out on what might be the last nice weekend of the year for being outside. This time of year in Missouri, the weather could change on you suddenly and there could be snow on the ground the following weekend. Just as likely, a sudden warm spell could pass through with record high temperatures. Rebecca was familiar with the uncertainties of a Missouri autumn and wasn't taking chances.

In the back of her mind, she admitted that fishing would give her an opportunity to think and maybe she would finally be able to sort out some of the chaos that was going on in her head. Sometimes she felt like she was spinning her wheels, yet she knew she was taking steps that should keep her life moving forward. She was more than halfway through her first semester of classes at the community college in Rockford where she attended morning classes and worked a work-study job in the afternoon. Deciding on a major was a task she had deemed currently impossible, so she was taking the basics toward an Associate of Arts degree until she could figure out what she really wanted to do with her life. Her tentative plan was to move to a larger university after a couple of years. The thought of this frightened her some, especially when she tried to imagine life away from the farm.

Rebecca crossed the fence into the second pasture, picked up her things from where she had pushed them under the fence and continued her hike. While she doubted she could be happy staying in this small area all of her life, she also dreaded the thought of leaving a place where she knew everyone and was known by everyone. She had grown up as the middle grandchild in a generational group of forty-five, most of them living within a twenty-mile radius. For several generations, her father's family had lived in the area, so distant cousins lived in all of the surrounding communities. The feeling that someone was watching out for her was ever-present and no one was a stranger. Sometimes life here felt stifling but usually it just felt good to know you always belonged. This secure feeling was something she knew she would have to leave behind.

As she crossed the second pasture she glanced over at the old Peacock Cemetery in the northwest corner of the pasture. There hadn't been a burial there for years and some of her school friends claimed it was haunted, not too much of a worry on a bright sunny morning. Something seemed different about the cemetery today though, and she stopped to really look for a few seconds. The gate had been hanging crooked for years but it had been closed and latched two weeks ago when she had last cut through the pasture on foot. *Maybe someone was up here fooling around on Halloween.*

She and her father had talked about fixing up the old cemetery someday, maybe putting a new fence around it and leveling up the ground. No one was caretaker for the cemetery anymore and people only visited it in attempts to see a ghost. Rebecca felt it was a shame that all of those interred there had been forgotten by the world.

As she walked up to the gate, she was afraid she would see vandalism. Instead she saw a fresh mound of dirt in front of an old headstone. The inscription on the stone was nearly worn away by the weather but by kneeling close to it she could make it out.

MARY J. FARTHING
March 1, 1907 – February 3, 1933

"Sad. She was so young." Rebecca spoke quietly but her voice sounded much louder in the still morning air. *Only eight years older than me.* She stood and looked around for any other signs of disturbance to the cemetery. The loose dirt near the mound revealed a couple of different shoe prints and the grass was trodden down around the headstone and in a path to the gate but the rest of the cemetery looked as if a human had not been there for many years. Her curiosity nearly got the best of her as she considered looking for a stick to loosen the dirt so she could move it aside and discover whether something had been hidden there. Her curiosity was stifled as she recalled her father's warnings about cave-ins of old graves. As she walked back out the gate, she stopped to carefully close it. She picked up her tackle box and pole then turned to walk away.

Her attention was captured by broken and leaning grass in two parallel lines outside the fence. She recognized them as tire tracks and they headed from the cemetery in a gentle curve until they were out of sight around a small grove of trees. A memory of headlights on Halloween night returned to her and she knew immediately this was where the lights had been. She assumed the old lane the tracks followed came out beside the old house she knew was down the road from her uncle's house. She thought about following the tracks but decided against it, heading on her way after latching the crooked gate, her thoughts still preoccupied with the fresh mound of dirt.

The area of disturbed dirt wasn't large enough for a coffin, not even a very small one. Maybe a shoe box or something that size could have been buried there, maybe even a small, beloved pet. But Mary Farthing had died in 1933 and surely there weren't any pets, even parrots, that could outlive their owners by more than eighty years.

Rebecca wasn't even sure there would be anyone around who would remember Mary Farthing. She decided she would take another walk that day, after fishing of course. Her grandmother lived past her house about a mile and might have some ideas.

* * *

Rebecca's first cast set the tone for the day. She immediately snagged her line on an old post at the bottom of the pond, left over from when a fence had divided the pond in half. "Shit!" she said loudly as she snapped her line. She tried to avoid cussing for her mother's sake but she enjoyed being able to let go and say what she felt when she was out of earshot of others. She quickly slipped the end of the line through the eye of another hook and tied it into place with practiced fingers then used needle-nose pliers from the tackle box to squeeze a couple of split-shot weights onto the line above the hook. The small knife she always carried in her pocket trimmed the end of the line. Then she baited her hook and tried again.

She caught a couple of small catfish, but mostly her bait fed the fish. Her attention was not on the vibrations coming through her line as the fish nibbled the worms or liver from her hook, but on that mysterious pile of freshly overturned dirt at Mary Farthing's grave. Early in the afternoon, she gave up on fishing. Feeling generous, she threw the remainder of the liver into the pond for a free meal for the fish if they could beat the turtles to it. She wasn't sure if she would get back to the pond before spring and she knew her mother wouldn't allow her to keep the old liver in her freezer until then. As far as moms go, her mother was pretty understanding, but she knew better than to push her luck.

She gathered up her things, including the empty chip bag and Vienna sausage can from which had come lunch. The Vienna sausages were a common meal for her when fishing, a tradition started by her father when he first began taking her to the river. Rebecca realized as she started the trek back toward her house that she hadn't spent any of her fishing time as planned, thinking about where her life was headed.

She walked back across the fields, turning south after dropping her tackle and pole behind the barn at her house. If she took them to the house, her mother might want to go along and then they would have to drive. Rebecca was enjoying her time alone, walking through the cool, crisp autumn air. Her reverie was interrupted by a piece of tin clanging loudly where it had pulled free from the screws that held it in place on the back corner of the barn roof. Rebecca made a mental note to tell her father about it before the wind caught it and carried it off into the field. She cut across the back pasture behind the barn to the county road on the other side, climbed over the fence and followed the dusty gravel road to her grandmother's house.

Grandma was her father's mother but nearly everyone around, relative or not, called her by that name. She was a head shorter than Rebecca but her personality was larger than life and she was the toughest woman Rebecca had ever met. Her nine children were all grown, with children and grandchildren of their own, but Rebecca knew they would all bow to her will if she exerted it. She usually opted to let them live their own lives and only used her power if she were really upset about something, like the time Uncle Fred forbade Aunt Jean from giving their daughter a baby shower because she wasn't married. By the time Grandma had finished with him, Uncle Fred had stepped meekly in line and even grilled burgers and hot dogs for all the ladies who attended the shower.

On the outside, Grandma appeared to be the typical gray-haired country grandma, wearing glasses, black SAS shoes and usually with a hint of something she had cooked that day adorning the front of her favorite duster. Behind that clever disguise was a combination teacher, psychologist, doctor and mind reader. Rebecca didn't think Grandma was afraid of anything, especially letting her feelings show, including showing you where you stood with her. Rebecca suspected that was why everyone loved her so much. She wished she had that same fearlessness but she tended to be more like her Dad, self-contained and less expressive when it came to emotions.

Grandma saw her walking up the sidewalk and came to the door to meet her. She grabbed Rebecca on either side of her face as she came into the house. Rebecca felt the skin of her cheeks tighten as she was pulled down to Grandma's height for a bear hug. It was hard to breathe when she squeezed you but the intensity of the hug told you to never doubt how much she loved you.

"Are you keeping out of trouble?" Grandma asked when she finally released her from her bone-squeezing grip.

"No, are you?" This was always asked and answered the same way. Grandma said she had so many kids that she was always in trouble with one of them. Rebecca was at the age where some of her older cousins really had been in trouble a time or two, whether from minor offenses such as staying out too late, skipping class or missing work, or more serious brushes with the local police over drag racing through town. She had the reputation in her family of being squeaky clean and she thought it actually concerned Grandma that she hadn't gotten into any trouble, so she always pretended that she had. Grandma knew the truth and knew her grandchildren better than they knew themselves.

"What have you been up to today?" Grandma asked, sitting down in her favorite recliner.

"I went fishing over in Uncle Jim's pond for a while but didn't catch anything. On the way, I walked past the old Peacock Cemetery. I noticed someone had disturbed some dirt around a grave there. It belonged to a Mary Farthing. Do you remember her?"

Grandma's sparkling blue eyes would get a cloudy, distant look when she thought back many years and today she looked like she was really searching to find a memory.

"She lived with her parents in that old two-story farmhouse that sits by where the lane turns down to the cemetery. I think she moved to the city when she was in her early twenties although I was pretty young at the time, so I might be wrong."

Rebecca knew her grandmother was talking about St. Louis. Everyone in the area just referred to it as "the city."

"She was still a young woman when she died. I recall there was a lot of secrecy about her death. Her folks went to the city on the train and brought her body back for a private funeral, family only. No one really ever knew what happened. There were a lot of illnesses at that time, so we supposed she had caught something and it upset her family to talk about it. She was their only child, except for maybe an infant who had died very young. You know, we were raised that you didn't ask questions. If people wanted you to know something they would tell you. The Farthings didn't talk about it so nobody asked, nobody knew exactly what had happened. It wasn't but a few years later that her folks sold the place and moved closer to the city too."

Rebecca was thinking aloud. "Well, if she didn't have any family around then who could have been messing around with her grave?"

"Are you sure it wasn't a molehill or maybe one of those armadillos dug a hole then filled it in again?"

"I don't think so, Grandma. Armadillos and moles don't pat down the dirt with shovels. I saw footprints around where they'd been digging and tire tracks in the tall grass on the lane to the cemetery where they'd driven in and back out again."

"Well, Bec, you're always looking for something to think about. Looks like you've got something to occupy you for a while. Let me know if I can help any more."

"Okay, Grandma. Thanks. I love you," Rebecca said as she hugged Grandma good-bye.

* * *

Sunday morning, Rebecca sat staring into her coffee wondering what she would bury in an old grave on Halloween night. So far all she had conjured up were ideas for pranks. She heard her father clear his throat and turned away from the black depths of her cup, surprised to see both her mother and father looking at her expectantly. Rebecca had always been a bit of a dreamer and this wasn't the first time they had caught her when her mind was wandering far from its present location. She should have been used to the look of mild irritation in their eyes when it happened, but she wasn't.

"I'm sorry," she apologized sincerely. "What did you say?"

"I asked how your classes are going." Her father didn't involve himself in her studies much, although he had quizzed her in history a few times in high school to help her prepare for tests.

Throughout most of Rebecca's life her father had seemed content to remain quiet while a houseful of females moved around him like miniature whirlwinds. Now that both of her sisters were married and no longer living at home, he had slowly become more vocal. It still surprised her when she found herself in a real conversation with him. Even when they worked together on the farm, he was often silent. Sure, he taught her how to use equipment and tools. He taught her about the livestock and the hay. But all of this was completed with a paucity of words.

The exception to this was when he was telling a story. He had a real gift for telling a tale. She and her sisters had always chosen him over their mother to read them a bedtime story. In his deep voice he would be the troll under the bridge, or he would adopt a falsetto tone as the three pigs sang out to taunt the wolf. His blue eyes would sparkle and he would laugh with delight as he entertained an always captivated audience.

"Classes are going fine, Dad. I did well on my mid terms."

"I went by Grandma's last night on my way home. She said you'd been by."

"Yeah. I had a few questions I wanted to ask her about Peacock Cemetery. When I walked past it yesterday on my way over to Uncle Jim's, I noticed someone had been messing around with a grave there."

Her parents exchanged worried looks. "What do you mean?" her father asked.

"It looked like something small had been buried over a grave, right up next to the marker."

"Could you read the name on the grave?"

"Mary Farthing. She died in 1933."

"I don't remember any Farthings," her dad said. He looked at Beth but she shook her head also.

"Grandma said they used to live in the old house just past the cemetery."

Her father nodded. "It's been abandoned for at least thirty years. I don't remember the names of any of the people who lived there when I was a kid, but nobody ever lived there for long." His eyes sparkled as he continued, "Must have been the ghost that ran them off." He lifted his shaggy eyebrows in mock horror.

Rebecca smiled at his expression. "On Halloween night I saw headlights out my bedroom window and I think they were coming from the cemetery. You could see where someone had driven down to it. It just doesn't make sense to me what someone would be burying at such an old grave."

"Hard to tell. It's a wonder it didn't cave in on them. Those old graves can collapse like a sink hole, Rebecca, and next thing you know, you're in the coffin with the corpse. Pretty gruesome, huh?"

Rebecca shuddered at the thought. "Sure would be a lot easier to figure out what's buried there if we could just dig it up," she hinted, hoping her father would think of a way for her to do just that without falling in.

"It's not safe, Bec. Promise me you won't be digging around that old grave," he ordered.

"Don't worry, Dad. I won't," she said dejectedly, thinking her chances of ever solving her little mystery were slim-to-none.

CHAPTER THREE

Sitting in her college algebra class Monday morning, Rebecca was in the same time zone but decades away from the polynomials on the blackboard. She had excelled in math in high school and much of her current class was a review of her advanced classes of the previous two years so there was little to keep her attention.

On the bulletin board in the hallway before class she had seen a notice about the local Genealogical Society. They were having their monthly meeting that evening at six. She thought that might be a good place to ask a few questions or look for some clues about the Farthings. Work ended at five-thirty so she would have time to grab a bite to eat and get to the old courthouse in time for the meeting.

The old courthouse was an historic building, which in Rebecca's opinion meant tall ceilings, cold, drafty rooms, poor lighting and hard, uncomfortable seats. When she entered the room where the Genealogical Society met, it was exactly what she had expected. There were several tables arranged in a square around the center of the room surrounded by folding metal chairs. She had expected to find a group dominated by older women and was surprised to see only three people she thought were sixty or older, two women and a man. Six of those seated around the square of tables were probably between thirty and sixty, and two men and four women comprised this group. Rebecca was relieved to see there were even two young women present who appeared to be close to her own age. One sat next to two other women and the resemblance between them led Rebecca to believe they were probably three generations from the same family, most likely grandmother, mother and daughter.

She turned her focus to the other young woman who was sitting at one corner of the square, away from the others who were busily chatting. Partially hidden in the dim light by shadows from the stacks of books that surrounded her, she was intently scanning the pages of a thick volume lying open on the long table in front of her.

Rebecca pulled out the chair closest to her. "Hello. I'm Rebecca, or Bec, if you like," she said politely.

The dark brown head slowly tilted up as if unsure to whom the greeting was directed. She looked distracted as she slowly scanned the room, finally stopping and appearing surprised as she saw Rebecca standing beside her. Rebecca was equally surprised, unprepared that such a beautiful face would be revealed to her when the young woman looked up. Short, curly hair framed a stunning smile. Reading glasses perched at the tip of her perfect nose, and dazzling green eyes peeked over the top of them.

"Oh, I'm sorry. I didn't hear you walk up. What was that you were saying?" she responded to Rebecca's greeting in a soft-but-sure voice. She blinked a few times and her smile deepened as she did a once-over of the tall, lanky young woman who was gazing curiously down at her.

"Hello. My name is Bec...Rebecca. You look pretty interested in something there." She indicated the book on the table.

"Yeah, I guess. It's probably just a wild goose chase. I'm sorry for being so rude. My name is Olivia," she said as she offered her hand, which Rebecca promptly reached out to shake.

Rebecca was surprised to find her hand tingling when Olivia's hand made contact with it. *Must be static in the air. Hope I didn't shock her.*

She sat down in the chair beside her and scooted up to the table. "Are you from around here?" she asked, unsure why but not wanting their conversation to end.

"Oh, well," Olivia hesitated a little as if deciding how much she wanted to divulge of herself and her reasons for coming to the meeting. "I am from so many places that I guess I'm from everywhere. I grew up in a military family so we moved a lot, and every time my dad deployed, Mom took us to one of The Greats to stay."

At Rebecca's puzzled look, she explained. "You know, great uncles and aunts, we just called them The Greats to make it easier."

Rebecca started to respond but was interrupted by movement from the other side of the room.

One of the middle-aged men stood, introduced himself as the President of the Genealogical Society and started the meeting by introducing its members. He then asked the others present to stand and introduce themselves as well as give a brief summary of their genealogical ties to the area. Olivia and Rebecca were the only two present who were not members and Rebecca looked pleadingly at Olivia to go first.

Olivia stood, obviously confident after years of moving to new places and meeting strangers. "I am Olivia Harmon." She spoke clearly while looking around the room at the members. "My father's family ties are all in Oregon but my mother's great-grandparents were from St. Louis. I have been working on some missing branches of my mother's family tree and I remembered that several years ago a great-aunt had mentioned some family connection in this county so I decided to come here and investigate. I saw your meeting date listed on your Web site, so here I am."

She sat down and gave Rebecca a smile of confidence. Rebecca hated speaking in front of groups, especially groups of strangers. She gulped and stood. "I'm Rebecca Wilcox. My family settled in the next county east before the Civil War and the next generation came into this county." She could see several of the members nodding, knowing there were generations of Wilcoxes in the county. By the time she gave the name of her parents and grandparents, they all appeared to recognize her links to the area. She didn't bother tracing out the family tree any further but ended by saying she was investigating land ownership in the county around the early 1900's for a paper for one of her college classes. She looked relieved as she took her seat again, thankful that no one had questioned her quick fabrication which had sounded like a lame excuse to her, but was unquestionably more plausible than someone investigating a mound of dirt in an old cemetery.

By the end of the meeting, Rebecca had learned of several resources available through the Genealogical Society and at the local library which could be useful for her. After the meeting officially ended, she and Olivia spent an hour searching through some of the materials the Society made available to them, including documents on land ownership, local club memberships from decades past and cemetery listings.

Rebecca usually found it difficult to be around strangers. Growing up in a small town, going to school with the same bunch of kids, she wasn't used to being around someone she didn't know. Surprisingly she found it easy to work beside Olivia. They settled into a relaxed companionship as they followed their individual paths through the available material. Rebecca looked up a couple of times to catch Olivia looking at her with a soft smile on her lips. She would smile back then return to her work, warmed if not puzzled by the exchange. Occasionally, their hands would make contact as they reached for books from the common pile between them and Rebecca noticed the same tingle with each contact.

Finally, they had exhausted the texts available for research and both had several pages of notes. Rebecca had a busy week ahead with school and work, so she knew she would probably not get to do more research until the weekend.

As they picked up their notebooks and headed outside, she asked Olivia, "Where do you go to college?"

"Oh, St. Louis University," Olivia answered quickly. "I'm in my second year, majoring in English literature. What about you? Didn't you say you were in college too?"

"Yeah," Rebecca said. "I just started at the community college here in Rockford but plan to transfer after a year or two, when I know what I want to study."

"Still undecided, huh?"

"Yeah. It's not that I'm not interested in any certain area," she explained. "It's more like I'm interested in too many different areas to make up my mind."

"Well, a lot of people change their minds after they pick a major, so maybe it's better to wait until you're sure before you take too many classes you may not need."

Rebecca was encouraged that Olivia agreed with her. It was a subject that she and her mother had frequently and contentiously discussed, with her mother urging her to make a decision and with no resolution between the two sides.

"So, are you coming back to hit the local library next or did you find all you needed?"

Olivia looked a little disappointed as she admitted, "I found a few leads but not what I was really looking for. I have to go back to St. Louis tonight and won't be able to return until Saturday. I skipped out on a class to be here today and had a friend take notes for me, but I need to be there the rest of the week."

Rebecca brightened. "I was planning on going to the library Saturday too. Let me give you my number and maybe we can meet and help each other out."

Olivia was smiling as she punched Rebecca's number into her cell phone, then immediately called her so that Rebecca would have her number also. As she turned to get into her car, Olivia turned to her with an enigmatic smile. "You know, I had thought that maybe tonight was a waste of time but now I think maybe it was more productive than I originally thought." She held up the phone, then slid into the car, winked at Rebecca and drove away, leaving Rebecca to puzzle over her words.

* * *

It had been a busy week with classes and work taking most of Rebecca's time. Despite all of the other demands on her time, she had been able to review the information she had gathered the night of the meeting. The book of cemeteries for the county had shown Mary Farthing and an infant Farthing with a birthdate two years after Mary's birthdate both buried in the small cemetery. However, she had not found other Farthings in any of the cemeteries in the book, which was consistent with Grandma's memories of the family moving out of the area.

She had looked through copies of old deeds from that township and had discovered the one for the property near the cemetery where the house was located. The property had been owned by John and Elizabeth Farthing from July 21, 1905, through March 30, 1938. This also matched with Grandma's recollection of the Farthings leaving the area after Mary's death. All her digging and searching had failed to find any more information about the Farthing family either before or after those dates. Rebecca looked forward to going to the library Saturday to look for more information.

When she was being honest with herself, she admitted she was also looking forward to seeing Olivia again. Since starting college, Rebecca still hadn't made many new friends. She still met with Sandy and sometimes one or two others of her old friends every month or two, but they lived further away from Rockford than she did. And most of her time now was spent in Rockford. Many of her friends had moved from the area anyway, either going away to college or chasing jobs or men in bigger towns.

Thinking back through her senior year, she realized there had been a distance growing between her and her friends for a long time, she just wasn't sure why and whether it was they who were changing or her, or both. While her friends were caught up in cruising, dating, engagements, wedding plans after graduation or going to the college closest to their boyfriends, Rebecca had skirted the edges of it all, spending more time with the sophomores or even the teachers. It seemed like her friends were living in a different world and what they did seemed to make sense to them but it sure didn't make sense to her. From her perspective most of her friends were following the same paths as the parents they liked to complain about so much. She loved her parents but knew she wouldn't be content with the same lives they had. But, she also knew she needed to learn more about herself and the world around her before she understood what would make her content.

Maybe that was another reason, aside from career uncertainty, that she had opted for the local community college. She'd been in the top five in her high-school class and had received partial scholarships at several public and private universities but by staying at home and by paying the lower tuition of the local school she was able to save money. Also, by taking general classes, she was learning about a variety of things and could learn more about people, life and, most importantly, herself before choosing a career.

Olivia struck her as someone she could learn from. Her background was different from anyone Rebecca had grown up with and she seemed unafraid of doing things that weren't cool. None of Rebecca's friends from high school would have been caught dead at a Genealogical Society meeting regardless of the reason. Olivia also seemed to exude self-confidence, like she knew a secret about life that Rebecca had yet to learn. This intrigued her and she eagerly waited for Saturday morning to arrive.

Friday after classes, Rebecca had a thirty-minute break before her work-study job started. She texted Olivia, "Still on 4 Sat?"

She was pleased to receive an immediate response, "10 ok?"

Rebecca quickly typed in her response, "c u at library at

10:)" As an afterthought, she immediately sent another message, "how about pizza 4 lunch?"

Olivia sent back her reply, "it's a date:)"

CHAPTER FOUR

Rebecca was up early Saturday. She threw in a load of laundry before breakfast then washed dishes and cleaned the kitchen before her mother could even ask. Her mother was a part-time counselor and teacher at a school for troubled boys in a town on the other side of Rockford. If she had a busy week, she often allowed some of the housework to accumulate until the weekend. On those occasions, she expected Rebecca to pitch in a little more. Before today, Rebecca always had to be prodded and usually several times.

"Wow! What's gotten into you this morning?" her mother queried, giving her a sideways glance around the edge of her newspaper. Rebecca looked at her mother, sitting at the kitchen table still in her robe and slippers with her hair maniacally twisted around her head, and wondered if the boys at the school would ever take her seriously if they could see her at home like this. She shook her head, knowing better than to speak her thoughts aloud.

"I arranged to meet Olivia Harmon today at ten at the Rockford library. Didn't want to keep her waiting," Rebecca explained.

"She's the girl from St. Louis, right? That means you're still obsessing over the cemetery thing. I'd forgotten about that. Well, while you're in town, can you pick up a few things for me?" As usual her mother didn't wait for a response but set her paper down and picked up a pad and pen from the center of the table to jot down a short list, knowing Rebecca hated to shop but would do it for her anyway, even when she gave that exasperated sigh and rolled her eyes like she was doing now.

"Okay, but I don't know what time I'll be back," Rebecca replied.

"How long can you spend looking at old books in the library? Or do you have other plans too?" her mother prodded.

"No. Well, pizza when we're done. I thought I might offer to show Olivia around if there are places she finds in her research that she wants to see."

Rebecca pulled up her insulated bib overalls over her jeans and flannel shirt then checked her pockets for her knife. She often needed it to cut the netting free from the bale of hay when she fed the cows. After grabbing her jacket and gloves, she snatched the tractor key from its spot on the rack. "I'll be back in a few minutes. I'll get your list then."

* * *

While Rebecca fed the cattle, her mother made her shopping list then stood in the back doorway watching her daughter on the tractor. It seemed to her that she was becoming a distant spectator in her daughter's life, sitting up in the nosebleed seats and all she could do was watch her through binoculars, not knowing how to get close enough to actually help her. Even if she could bridge the growing distance, she wasn't sure how to advise her youngest one, how to make things easier for her, so she did the only thing she knew to do: watch and wait for an opportunity to close the gap and stay prepared in case she was needed.

At the boys' school where she worked, she watched the students try to set their course in life, some more successfully than others. Many of them turned to her for advice or support but some were fiercely independent and all she could do was watch and wait, hoping they would come to her if they needed her. Over the years she had witnessed many of them make poor decisions that had set the tone for the remainder of their lives, too proud or too stubborn to accept her assistance. Her greatest fear was that Rebecca would do the same. When she saw Rebecca jump down from the tractor, she returned to the table to sit down with her paper again, not wanting her to know about her concern.

Rebecca burst back into the house with a blast of cold air following her. She removed the insulated bibs and exchanged the rubber boots for Nikes. She hung her old coat in the hall closet and pulled out the new hooded Carhartt coat she had purchased last month to wear when she wasn't working on the farm. It was heavy and not exactly dressy but her mother knew she was comfortable in it and she knew of no other coat which would keep her daughter warmer.

She took the list and two folded bills from her mother's outstretched hand, scanned the list quickly and shoved the thirty dollars into her front jeans pocket.

When she sensed Rebecca had turned to leave, Beth lowered the paper again, watching her retreating back. She was glad to see Rebecca this interested in something, even if it was a pile of dirt in an old graveyard. She had spoken with Rebecca several times about trying to narrow her focus on things, especially her career choices. But Rebecca seemed to jump from one thing to the next, quickly losing interest in one thing and moving on to a new topic with no warning. She would catch her sitting quietly at times with a strange look on her face, mulling over things, she supposed. Maybe the fact that she was actively following up on something that interested her was an indication that Rebecca was settling down a little and would be able to focus on things better.

* * *

It was ten-fifteen when Rebecca walked into the library. She had seen Olivia's car parallel parked in front of the building with an open spot at either end. Two years earlier, she had nearly flunked her driving test due to parallel parking and her Buick wasn't exactly economy-sized. Had there been two consecutive spots available she would have taken one, but instead she had circled around the building and parked her 1995 hand-me-down Buick in the angle parking lot behind the library. She wasn't sure she wanted to try parallel parking today, especially not with Olivia's car in danger from any mistakes she might make.

Rebecca walked past the small foreign car and took the library steps two at a time. *Olivia's car might be easier to park.*

The librarian directed her to an alcove of the building dedicated to local interests. She recognized one of the older women from Monday night's meeting sitting at a table near the window leafing through some papers. She was a little disappointed to not see Olivia right away, although she did see a notebook and pen on a small table in the center of the alcove. Nearby, a leather jacket was slung over the back of a chair and the thin strap of a small purse hung across it. The notebook looked like the one she had seen Olivia carrying the night of the meeting so she placed her notebook opposite it on the table and walked over to the nearest bookcase. After scanning the books, she pulled out a volume on early history of the county. Out of the corner of her eye, she noticed movement on the other side of the bookcase through the small gap left by the book she had extracted. She placed her face close to the bookcase and was startled to see an eye peering through at her. Below the eye, she saw one corner of a smile and couldn't help but chuckle as she said, "Olivia, I presume?"

"But, of course!" Olivia laughed as she replied. "You are late," she said, trying for a stern voice.

"Traffic slowed me down," was the best excuse Rebecca could find.

"Traffic must be really bad on Saturday mornings in a big city like Rockford." Olivia smiled mockingly at Rebecca as she rounded the end of the bookcase and approached her. "I thought you'd stood me up."

Even more beautiful than I remembered. Olivia's soft gray sweater clung softly to her breasts and her jeans fit her hips and thighs almost intimately. Rebecca realized she had been silent too long and struggled to remember what Olivia had said. *Oh, yeah. The traffic.*

Rebecca didn't want to admit she had been daydreaming on the way to the library. She had looked down twice and found herself going fifteen miles under the speed limit. Her mother would never believe it, she had thought at the time. Then she had missed the street to the library so she took the next street, which seemed to have a stop sign on every block. Unable to come up with a better excuse, Rebecca just smiled sheepishly and said questioningly, "Sorry?" Then, trying to quickly change the subject, she added, "So have you found anything interesting yet?"

Olivia chuckled. At her quick change of topic, Rebecca guessed. "I have found a few things that interest me." She smiled and Rebecca was sure she saw her wink before she turned to resume her search through the shelves. Olivia added over her shoulder to a confused Rebecca, "Let's get to work."

The next three hours passed quickly with Rebecca and Olivia searching the shelves for books and taking notes. The final half hour they were interrupted several times by rumbles beneath the table coming from the general direction of Olivia's stomach. Rebecca had been waiting for her to say something about stopping for lunch but after one especially loud growl she decided to speak up. "I'm ready for a break and it sounds like you are too."

Olivia pinked a little. "I was hoping you hadn't noticed. I'm ready for pizza if you are. I was just waiting for you to say when."

They agreed to take Olivia's car across town for lunch, leaving Rebecca's old Buick parked in the back. Olivia exclaimed several times her disbelief about the horrible traffic as she drove through virtually empty streets with Rebecca laughing easily at her own lame excuse.

At the pizzeria, they both ordered the buffet and cherry Cokes. Before they could leave the table to get their food, a woman in her mid-twenties approached and slid into the booth beside Rebecca, pushing her over next to the wall.

"Hi, kid. What are you doing here?"

Rebecca was surprised to see her sister, Kate. "Been studying at the library and decided to take a break for some lunch. Where's Jimmy?"

"Oh, he's up in line waiting to pay. I've got to go to work in about half an hour. By the way, I'm Bec's sister, Kate. My husband Jimmy's over there." She added the last as she stuck her hand out over the table toward Olivia.

"Oh, yeah. Sorry. Olivia, this is Kate. Kate, this is a friend of mine from St. Louis, Olivia Harmon." Rebecca was a little embarrassed by her own lack of manners but Olivia didn't seem to be bothered by her accidental omission. In fact, she appeared a little relieved, which Rebecca noticed but didn't quite understand.

* * *

Olivia shook Kate's hand briefly then sat back and studied the differences between the two sisters. Kate's hair was dyed blonde and cut short in a recent, popular style and she wore tastefully applied makeup. She was dressed in scrubs so Olivia assumed her job was in the medical field. Rebecca on the other hand had tousled hair from the breeze that had been blowing all morning and Olivia was sure the color was natural, brown with streaks of blonde from being in the sun. She wore no makeup and her face was tanned unevenly as if she had spent a lot of time outside with a ball cap shading part of her face and her forehead. She also looked comfortable in loose fitting jeans and a flannel shirt and Olivia had trouble picturing her in something more feminine. Their handshakes were even different, she realized. Rebecca's hand had been rough and calloused and her handshake firm but slightly hesitant, as if she wasn't sure how much of her strength she should display in a handshake. Kate's, in contrast, was firm and sure but her hand was much smoother and softer.

"Well, I guess I better run," Kate said. "Jimmy just finished paying."

Rebecca's tall, thin brother-in-law, with spiked blond hair, was heading for the door while scanning the room for his wife. Rebecca waved to him when his gaze passed over her, then playfully shoved Kate out of the booth. "See ya later, sis."

She and Olivia headed for the buffet, grabbed plates and filled them quickly. After stuffing themselves on pizza and breadsticks, they refilled their sodas then again returned to their booth.

"Is it just you and your sister or do you have more in your family?" Olivia asked after devouring her first piece of pizza.

"Kate is the oldest, then my sister June then me. I'm the baby." Rebecca's tone indicated her dislike for always being the youngest of the group.

"Just think," Olivia pointed out. "Being the youngest will be a good thing when you're older. They'll both be over the hill before you are." She smiled teasingly.

"I guess that's true but I hope it'll be awhile before I'm considered over the hill. Let me get through my first semester of college, at least." Rebecca smiled back at Olivia and Olivia noticed how much her mood had brightened.

"So how is your research going?" Rebecca asked.

"I've followed several leads but so far it's all been dead ends." Olivia played with the straw in her glass.

"Maybe I can help. I've lived here forever, you know. I would probably recognize a lot of names in the area. I could even take you driving around the area if you need a tour guide," Rebecca offered.

Olivia admitted, "I'm not sure where I would begin. I'm not even sure I'm looking for the correct names."

At Rebecca's puzzled expression, she explained. "You see,

there's something about my family that's a secret, even from me. It's got something to do with my great-grandmother. A few months ago I overheard my mother talking about it on the phone to her brother, my uncle Steve. She and my dad stayed in North Carolina when he retired from the military, but she flies to St. Louis two or three times a year to see us. She'd come to visit for a couple of weeks and she thought I was in my bedroom but I was lying down on the sofa and she couldn't see me from where she sat. She was saying that 'it was way overdue' and 'should have been taken care of years ago.' Several times she said Gran's name—that's what we called my great-grandma. Then she said it would have to be taken care of by them without my grandmother finding out, which would take some planning. She added that it was a shame they didn't go more often, she was family after all. I sneezed and she started asking questions about his work, my cousins, you know, normal stuff. When I asked her about it later, all she would say was it had to do with settling Gran's estate and she didn't want to talk about it because Grandmama, my grandmother, didn't like people dredging up the past."

Rebecca had been listening intently and was intrigued by Olivia's mystery. "What's the link to here?"

Olivia looked a little unsure as she continued, "Well, I'm probably grasping at straws but my mother won't tell me who she was talking about. There is, or was, more family around somewhere. I remember one of my great-aunts mentioning a link to this county once when I was much younger. I obviously can't ask Grandmama and she was the only child. My Gran had brothers and sisters. Remember we called them The Greats? But they're all gone now. Gran was ninety-nine when she died ten years ago. I never knew my great-grandfather. Grandmama told me he died very young and she had no memories of him. Even my grandfather died when I was little, so there's no one left to ask."

Olivia took a sip of her cherry Coke and continued her tale. "Last time I was at Grandmama's house I looked through all the photo albums to see if there was someone I didn't recognize.

I noticed there were no pictures of my great-grandfather. When I asked, Grandmama said there had been one but it must have been misplaced. I did find a photo of Gran when she was probably between twenty and twenty five years old standing beside another young woman of about the same age and a young man maybe a few years younger than them. I asked Grandmama if he was my great-grandfather and she laughed this really bitter-sounding laugh then said that picture showed the reason I never knew my great-grandfather. That's all she would say."

"Wow! I see what you mean about secrets." Rebecca was leaning forward over the table, caught up in the story Olivia was telling. "But, I still don't see what it has to do with here."

"I'm getting to that," Olivia continued. "After Grandmama had walked away, I looked at the back of the picture. It said, 'Jane, MJ and Ralph, Springtown, MO, April, 1929.' And that is what brought me here."

"Springtown!" Rebecca exclaimed, sitting up straight in her booth. "That's my hometown." She waited for Olivia to grasp the importance of this but Olivia just looked at her blankly.

"Living in a small town is a lot different than living in a city," Rebecca explained. "Someone in a small town knows something about everyone and everything that has ever happened in that small town. We just have to figure out who that someone is. Can you get a copy of that picture?" Rebecca asked.

Olivia was startled at Rebecca's question. "Well, yes, I guess. But, I don't see how that can help. I don't think you're old enough to recognize them," she added, teasingly.

"No, but I know a few people who might be." Rebecca smiled at Olivia encouragingly.

* * *

After making plans to meet again the following weekend, Olivia took Rebecca back to her car. Rebecca was reluctant to part company but knew Olivia still had a drive ahead of her and she still had shopping to do for her mother. Olivia also looked a little sad as she pulled up in the library's back parking lot beside Rebecca's old Buick.

Rebecca thought she must be disappointed about her research that day. "Don't worry," she said softly, reaching out and giving Olivia's hand a gentle squeeze. "We'll get this all figured out."

"Oh," said Olivia. "I'm not worried. I was just thinking about how much I enjoyed today and how I hate to go back to St. Louis. Thanks for the pizza, by the way."

"Any time," said Rebecca and she was surprised to realize how much she meant it. She had found such easy companionship with Olivia and was glad she was returning in one week. "Can you stay the weekend next time? Mom and Dad won't mind if you stay. Mom would probably welcome the chance to make me clean the guest bedroom." She groaned in mock despair, thinking of the things she would have to put away so the room could be used.

"Sure, I would love to stay," Olivia said softly with that funny smile Rebecca had seen a few times when she had caught Olivia looking at her, in the library, in the restaurant and in the car. "Too bad you don't have a place of your own yet."

Then Olivia quickly leaned over, gave Rebecca a quick hug, a kiss on the cheek then pushed away as she said, "Go now and I'll see you next weekend. Text me and we'll get the details set up."

Rebecca was too surprised by the show of affection to do more than respond with a quick good-bye as she slid out of the car, closed the door and watched Olivia pull away.

Her mind raced as she completed her mother's shopping. Olivia had gotten closer to her in just two days, not even full days at that, than most of her friends had done in weeks or months of knowing her. She guessed that was her own fault; she wasn't exactly overflowing with emotion most of the time. There was something different about Olivia though. There was no comparison between the night with her friends at the pizza place and today with Olivia. She had really enjoyed herself today instead of sitting on the outside looking in, wondering what was wrong. Typically when she was surrounded by her peers, she felt like she was in a foreign land. Somehow with Olivia it was like they spoke the same language. They were also both intrigued by a mystery. Rebecca had to admit that, in her mind, the pile of dirt at Peacock Cemetery had taken a backseat to Olivia's family secrets. She already knew two people she would take Olivia to visit and maybe they would lead her to others.

As she pulled into her driveway her phone alert sounded. Olivia had texted. "Made it home. Had a great day. Can't wait to c u again."

She texted Olivia back quickly, "Me 2," then hoisted the fifty-pound bag of dog food onto her shoulder, picked up the plastic shopping bag and her notebook in her other hand and headed into the house to tell her mother how her day had gone.

CHAPTER FIVE

It was Wednesday afternoon, sitting at the desk in the Resource Room at the school, when Rebecca put it all together. She was a smart girl, all of her teachers had been saying that for years. However, when it came to people, she sometimes missed the obvious. *Can't wait to see you again.* The text from Olivia hadn't said "looking forward to next weekend" or even "hope to find a lot of clues next week." It sounded so much more personal than that. When she had texted her back about the pizza, she had used the word "date." There had been a few things about Olivia that had puzzled her, like the wink she was sure she had seen in the library. And then there was that funny smile Rebecca kept seeing on her face when Olivia was watching her and she seemed to catch her watching her a lot. *Could Olivia be…? No… why would she be interested in me? Besides, that would mean Olivia was gay, or maybe lesbian would be the right word, or maybe even bisexual.*

Some of Rebecca's friends at school had talked about relatives that were gay and a boy in the class ahead of her had come out his senior year. And, of course, she watched *Ellen* and even *Rosie* every now and then, but somehow they didn't seem real to her. In the real world, in *her* small world, girl met guy, they fell in love, married, had a baby and life happened. Some people changed the sequence of events, some placed a college education into the equation somewhere, a few remained bachelors or, ugh, she hated the term, old maids. While she felt like a person ought to be able to live how they felt was right for themselves without other people trying to make those decisions for them, she really hadn't given much thought to those who lived their lives outside that basic outline.

Rebecca puzzled over Olivia every spare moment as she worked the desk at the Resource Room each day after classes, as she drove the thirty-minute trek to and from Rockford and as she sat at home with her parents, supposedly "studying" with a book in her lap or on the table in front of her. Her mother had to try three times to get her attention Thursday evening to tell her a neighbor's mother had passed away and she and Rebecca's father would be gone for a few hours after supper Saturday evening to attend the visitation at the funeral home in Rockford.

Friday brought a new revelation. Rebecca had been drinking coffee at breakfast with her mother, still mulling over the possible motivations behind Olivia's words and actions. Just as she took a sip of the steaming coffee, she switched her attention from Olivia to herself. She inhaled the coffee and began spluttering loudly when she realized that she might like the idea of Olivia being interested in her.

Rebecca's mother looked around the edge of her ever-present newspaper. "Are you okay, Bec?"

As soon as she could breathe again, she croaked out, "Yeah, Mom. Just went down the wrong pipe."

After a few more seconds of throat clearing and wiping the tears from her eyes, Rebecca settled down again and tried another sip, this one more successful.

Her mother placed her paper neatly on the table and caught Rebecca's eyes in her direct gaze. "Are you really okay, though?

You've been pretty distracted this week. Is school going okay? What about work?"

Rebecca was slow to reply, taking another sip of the scalding coffee to give herself time to come up with an answer. "Yes, I'm fine. Just thinking about the weekend," she admitted. She had decided a couple of years before that it was futile to lie to her mother. She always seemed to know the truth. But she wasn't ready to share the entire truth, that she had invited a girl to spend the night who very well may have been making passes at her. She needed to get her thoughts sorted out before she started working on sharing them with someone else, especially her mother.

"I gotta run," she said, putting her dishes in the sink. "Do you need anything from town?"

"No." Her mother stood from her chair at the table and grabbed Rebecca in a quick hug before she could get past her. "I love you, Bec."

"What was that all about?" Rebecca muttered to herself as she grabbed her books and headed out to the Buick. Not only was she having trouble recognizing herself, now her mother was acting weird, too.

* * *

The daydreams of Friday were dominated by one topic. *What am I going to do if she is interested in me...and if I'm interested in her?* Rebecca sometimes believed she could over-analyze things a bit but this was a pretty important topic, so she let herself go. *I think I kind of like the idea. Do I like it because someone is interested, because Olivia is interested, or because a woman is interested...or because I'm interested in her? If I like it because it's a woman, is that why I've never had a real boyfriend? Is that why I was totally distracted by my high-school English teacher's breasts my sophomore year, but never gave my math teacher a second glance, even though all my friends thought he was really hot? Surely I couldn't get this far in life without figuring out if I'm gay...lesbian or not.*

After going through her classes in a daze, Rebecca found her work-study boss and made an unusual request. She lied about having an upcoming test and asked for the afternoon off to study. She had made a pact with herself to try to always be honest but this was just going to have to be an exception. The clamor in her head was becoming deafening and she needed desperately to find a quiet place to sort it all out. Time was getting short. She had to figure something out before 10:30 Saturday morning, which was less than a day away.

By the time Rebecca had driven five miles out of town to Piney Creek, she was exhausted by the din in her head. She locked up the Buick and headed down the overgrown trail along the creek bank, looking out at the clear water drifting past. She loved the rivers and creeks in this part of Missouri and Piney Creek was pretty quiet this time of year. About a quarter mile from the trailhead was a large, flat-topped rock which jutted out over the current. She clambered up onto it and watched the water rush by, trying to quiet down her thoughts so she could concentrate on one idea at a time.

The water always seemed to have a calming effect on her and today was no different. It was almost like the current washed away all the chaff from her thoughts, allowing her to focus on what was important. After about an hour, she was starting to get a little chilled and her butt was getting sore from sitting on the hard, cold rock, but the clamor in her head had stilled. She walked back to the Buick feeling a little lighter than before, confident in her decision to be honest with herself and at least have the courage to find the answers, to discover what, or *who*, she did or didn't want. Self-deception or running from the unknown served her no purpose. A little courage was called for and she vowed to keep an open mind until she really knew how she felt. When she reached that point, she knew more courage might be necessary for her to act on her feelings, but she would worry about that when the time came.

Rebecca arrived home a little earlier than usual and her mother asked her about it as soon as she came in the front door.

"Oh, I took off work this afternoon. I can make it up over the next week by working my lunch break. I'll just take a PB&J sandwich and eat it at the desk." Rebecca knew this answer wouldn't satisfy her mother so she added, "I just needed some time to think so I went down to Piney Creek for a while."

"Well, did you solve the great questions of world peace, or feeding the hungry, or anything else with all of that thinking?" Her mother smiled as she reached out and tousled her hair.

Rebecca's face brightened a little as she laughed and replied, "Well, no. I guess I didn't solve anything that important. I guess my own personal turmoil can't be too important compared to world peace and famine."

"Care to share that personal turmoil, oh youngest daughter of mine?" her mother probed lightly, looking with worry at her daughter.

"I don't think I can right now, Mom," Rebecca answered as truthfully as she could. "I don't trust my thoughts right now. I need to figure out what I really think about things first." She paused a little, noticing her mother looked puzzled at her explanation. "I know I'm probably not making much sense, but I promise, Mom, I'll talk to you as soon as I think I can." Rebecca had no desire to push her away. At the same time, she knew this was something she was going to have to figure out on her own.

"Okay, I can wait. You know, I've found when I'm not sure what I think about something, if I really think about how I feel about it, deep in my heart, I come up with the answer. I don't know if that helps any, but it has for me. Rebecca, I'll be here if you need me, if there is any way I can help." She had placed her hands on both of Rebecca's shoulders and made sure Rebecca's eyes met hers as she said this.

"Now," her mother added, changing to a lighter tone. "Because you are home early, you win the grand prize…the privilege of helping me cook supper!" She linked one arm through Rebecca's and led her to the kitchen, where a paring knife and a pile of vegetables sat on the counter waiting for her attention.

CHAPTER SIX

The next morning, Rebecca felt jittery at breakfast. She was trying to act calm so her mother wouldn't ask more questions she didn't have answers for. She was glad her mother seemed to be letting things slide this morning, only asking, "So, what are you girls planning for today?"

"I'm meeting Olivia at the gas station in town then leading her back here. I thought I'd have her drop her car off here at the house then take her to Grandma's. We might go to Mrs. Wright's house after that. She seems to know a lot about people from way-back-when. I may even take her to see Peacock Cemetery."

"I may not be here when you drop her car off. I've got to go grocery shopping this morning. Your dad will be over at Uncle Jim's most of the day. Remember, it's deer season, so if you go out to the cemetery, take some orange with you so you don't get shot."

"Okay, I'll pull out a couple of blaze orange ball caps. When is Dad going hunting?"

"I think he plans to go early several mornings this week. Are you going to hunt this year?"

"I don't think so. I'm pretty busy with classes during the week and Olivia will be here this weekend. Besides, I haven't even bought a deer tag."

Rebecca had been excited about deer season ever since her father had taken her the first time when she was ten. She had never shot one but had seen several pass by, with no good shot available. Her father had taught her to hunt safely and to respect wildlife, so she would never take a shot carelessly and risk only injuring the deer, which she knew would lead to infection and suffering before the deer died days later. The deer population locally had grown over the past couple of decades and without hunting, the dangers of driving the roads around the area would be great and the deer would become unhealthy from too little food. She found hunting to be a challenge and enjoyed the venison from the deer her father had harvested. But, she was surprised to realize, she just had no desire to hunt this year. Her mind wasn't up to the challenge maybe, with all the other distractions she was dealing with.

"I'll do the dishes," Rebecca offered as she gathered their cups and plates from the table. She hoped having something to do would make the time pass faster.

"I think I like this new mood you've been in," her mother teased, watching her work for a few minutes before she returned to her paper.

* * *

Rebecca made sure she was fifteen minutes early when she got to the gas station that morning. She couldn't help but tease Olivia when she pulled in five minutes late. "Traffic heavy?" she asked, arching one eyebrow and trying to look serious.

Olivia smiled out the open car window. "I knew you'd have something to say about it," she laughed.

"Follow me and my trusty Buick and I'll take you to my house," Rebecca said as she handed Olivia a bottle of cherry Coke.

"What's this for?"

"I picked us both up a soda while I was waiting on you," Rebecca said. "That is what you had the other day, isn't it?"

"Yeah, you got it right. Thanks." Olivia smiled and winked and Rebecca felt herself blush a little, so she turned quickly and jogged across the lot to her car.

By the time they drove the two miles to her house, Rebecca felt like she had it all under control again but when Olivia slid into the front seat of the Buick, she felt her cheeks try to pinken. Desperate to divert Olivia's attention away from her unease, she blurted out, "So, how did you get the picture?"

Rebecca felt herself slowly relaxing as Olivia recounted how she had asked her grandmama if she could copy some old photos from her albums, then had slid out the one of MJ, Jane, and Ralph, and hid it behind the others. "I don't think Grandmama was any the wiser," she said confidently.

Rebecca pointed out to Olivia, as she drove to Grandma's, all the fields and pastures that belonged to either her father or Grandma. She also explained that most people around the area called her Grandma whether they were related or not and assured her that Grandma would want her to call her that, also, if she was comfortable doing so.

Rebecca was a little embarrassed when they entered Grandma's front door. She had forgotten to tell Olivia about the bear hug. She felt the familiar pull on her cheeks to get her down to Grandma's shorter stature, then she hugged Grandma as much as she could while being squeezed tightly. She was pleased to see Olivia receive the same treatment. Grandma had so many grandkids and other relatives that she treated anyone that came through her door like they were one of her own. Olivia didn't seem at all bothered by the familiarity and hugged Grandma back with equal affection.

After Rebecca introduced Olivia, Grandma interrupted, "So, are you two girls keeping out of trouble today?"

Rebecca had forgotten to explain this ritual, also, but responded with her typical answer. "No. How about you, Grandma?" This caused a lifted eyebrow from Olivia but she didn't ask questions. They spent the next thirty minutes laughing with Grandma about how she made this daughter mad about one thing and went somewhere with another one, which upset a third daughter, and on and on.

Grandma could make a dull week sound grand. You never knew quite what to expect from her and she had surprised Rebecca more than once. She hated playing cards, thought it was "the devil's work." She hated divorce, but just a few weeks before, she had told Rebecca, "I think it's better to try someone out for a while to see if you can get along than it is to marry them, then find out you can't stand to look at them over the breakfast table."

Rebecca loved it when Grandma shared her thoughts with her, but was sure some of her thoughts were why she was always in trouble with one daughter or another. Grandma wasn't one to hide her feelings and Rebecca knew Grandma would speak up at times when she would have chosen to let things settle down a little. But that was also one of the things Rebecca most loved and respected about her.

Finally, Grandma said, "Tell me about yourself, Olivia. Is your family from this area?"

Olivia quickly explained about her army brat upbringing, her parents retiring in North Carolina, her father's family in Oregon, and her mother's family from St. Louis. Then she pulled out the copy of the old photo and showed it to her. "Do you recognize any of these people?" she asked.

Grandma studied the picture intently for a few minutes. "I don't believe I can tell you who they are. I'm not even sure where it was taken, but the house in the background does look familiar. I just can't place it right now."

Rebecca looked at the picture over Grandma's shoulder. She hadn't thought to look at the background. "You're right, Grandma. That house does seem familiar, but I can't think of where I've seen it. Maybe Ola Wright will know. We're planning on taking it to her next. Is there anyone else you can think of who might recognize someone or something in the picture?"

"If Ola Wright isn't able to help you, I don't think anyone could. When she was a younger woman, she knew everything about everyone in these parts," she added with a smile. "But, if I think of something that will help you girls, I'll give you a call."

"Thanks, Grandma," Rebecca said as she hugged her good-bye.

"Yes. Thank you, Grandma," Olivia echoed, giving her a tight hug. "It was very nice to meet you. I hope I get to see you again, soon."

"I enjoyed meeting you, too. Don't be a stranger. You can come to see me anytime," Grandma said sincerely. "Now, you take my granddaughter and go see what kind of trouble you can get her into."

She shooed them out the door then stood in the doorway waving while Rebecca headed the Buick back up the road toward town.

"I love your grandma," Olivia exclaimed. "She is so…real. I mean, she's nothing like my grandmother. You're lucky to have such a wonderful person in your life."

Rebecca hadn't considered it, but she did feel pretty blessed to have been born into her family. "I agree completely," she said.

Mrs. Wright wasn't able to help them out and they were both a little dejected as they left her house. She had suggested they drive around to see if they could spot the house from the picture. Their optimism had been damaged that much more when she pointed out the house may not be standing anymore.

Rebecca, trying to stay positive, suggested they drive down each street in Springtown. The streets were basically aligned in a grid pattern with seven streets running north and south, eight running east and west. It wouldn't take long to see the entire town.

The old Buick putt-putted along the narrow streets as Rebecca pointed out the highlights of town. There weren't many, and most people probably wouldn't call them highlights, but they were the hubs of what little activity this town ever saw. There was the post office, the beauty shop, four churches, two gas stations, the small general store and the volunteer fire department with a flashing sign in front advertising their bluegrass singing the second Saturday of every month, and where numerous benefits had been held for local residents in times of need.

Olivia was intrigued by the makeup of the little town. "Four churches! Isn't that a little much for a town this small? And there aren't any bars. I thought every town had a bar."

"The old tavern building is on the north end of town but it's been deserted for years. I heard Dad say the other day someone was planning to tear it down. And there's a place south of town that was a bar for a while but someone remodeled it and is living in it now. People just drive to Rockford or Freedom if they want a bar. As far as the churches go, there used to be five. I guess even though there may be fewer people in a small town, there are still a lot of different ways of thinking about things," Rebecca speculated.

"I can agree with having different ways of thinking about things," Olivia said, with a sideways glance at Rebecca.

Rebecca felt a little skip in her heartbeat and a little flush crept into her cheeks but she was able to say, in what she hoped was a normal tone, "Yeah, me too."

They finished the streets in town and were back at Rebecca's house by one o'clock. "Just in time for lunch," her mother greeted them as they came in the door. "Olivia, I presume? I'm Beth, or Mom, whichever you'd like to call me. I have three daughters who call me Mom, so one more won't be a problem. Girls, sit down at the table," she continued, not giving Olivia a chance to respond. "I just mixed up some chicken salad for sandwiches. I'm making lunch for Dad and Uncle Jim but there is plenty. I was hoping you'd run it over to them when you've finished your lunch, Rebecca, if you're not too busy. They're bush-hogging the field behind the catfish pond."

"Bush hogging?" Olivia asked as she sat down at the table.

Rebecca gathered plates and made sandwiches as her mother explained the machinery and techniques used to clear brush from the rolling, rocky pastures of the Ozarks. Rebecca's mother and Olivia chatted easily throughout the meal, giving Rebecca a chance to sit back and reflect on the morning. It had been a good morning and Rebecca believed she had enjoyed every minute since Olivia had driven into the parking lot at the gas station.

"Rebecca!" her mother said loudly.

Rebecca jumped as she realized she had been ignoring the conversation between her mother and Olivia while she drifted in her thoughts. "Yes. I'm here. What did you say?"

"I know you're here, dear. I was just saying to be back for an early supper at five. Dad and I have that visitation to go to tonight and we want to leave by six, at least," her mother reminded her.

"Okay, sounds good. Well, Olivia, shall we take Dad and Uncle Jim their lunch?" Rebecca looked over at Olivia, who was smiling that funny smile at her again.

Her mother quickly gathered the sandwiches in a bag and handed Olivia the jug of tea. "See you at five. Oh, and don't forget your blaze orange."

"Got it, Mom," Rebecca said as she grabbed the orange hats from the hat rack by the back door.

"Thanks for lunch, Mom," Rebecca and Olivia chimed together, then laughed as they headed out the door.

"What's up with the hats?" Olivia asked as they headed for the car.

"Oh, it's rifle hunting season for deer and Mom worries we'll get shot going out in the field without some blaze orange on to warn the hunters."

"But, I'll mess up my hair." Olivia pretended to pout, sticking out her lower lip a little, but was unable to prevent a laugh.

"Too bad," Rebecca answered with mock seriousness. "Mother has spoken."

It was a short drive around the pastures to Uncle Jim's house where Rebecca had fished just two weeks before. Aunt Patsy was in St. Louis visiting their oldest daughter for a couple of days so the house and the yard were empty when they pulled up. Rebecca saw her father's truck sitting across the field and could hear the tractor running in the distance. "Guess we'll walk from here," she said. "If that's okay, I mean."

"I would love to walk with you," said Olivia, climbing out of the Buick with the jug of tea in hand.

Rebecca tossed her one of the hats from the dashboard and laughed as Olivia placed it on her head. Instead of fitting snugly against her head, it nestled at an angle atop unruly curls which sprang unevenly from beneath the edges. She could tell Olivia wasn't used to wearing a ball cap but its awkward placement somehow made her look even more beautiful. She slapped her own cap on her head, familiar with the feel of it, immediately comfortable with its fit. She grabbed the sandwiches and pushed the door shut with her hip then walked to the front of the car to join Olivia for the hike into the field.

"That's my dad standing over by the truck." Rebecca pointed as they drew nearer. A tall, graying man stood behind the truck, his attention captured by a chainsaw resting on the tailgate in front of him. His jeans were faded and patched and as they watched, he rubbed his hand over the side of his pant leg, leaving long streaks of black to mingle with the faded stains from days past. "Mom won't let him ruin a good pair of jeans so she patches the old ones until there's nothing left to hold the patches together," Rebecca explained.

"Dad, we brought lunch," she yelled.

He turned at the sound of her voice, spying them immediately and smiling a warm welcome. He wiped his hand on his pant leg again as he walked toward them, reaching his hand out to Olivia before Rebecca could introduce her. "You must be Olivia," he said with a slight country drawl. "I'm Willie, Rebecca's dad."

Olivia smiled and took his hand. "It's nice to meet you, Mr. Wilcox."

"No. Call me Willie or Dad, please. Don't make me feel any older than I already do." He placed his hand over Rebecca's ball cap and turned it sideways. "This one already makes me feel old. Seems like yesterday she was climbing up my leg trying to steal the change out of my pants pockets. Now look at her."

Rebecca thought about just pulling the ball cap down over her face instead of straightening it on her head. "Dad," she warned and he smiled mischievously.

"Bec, run out and flag down your Uncle Jim while Olivia and I talk."

She thought about protesting but finally decided she and Olivia would be able to leave more quickly if she just did what he asked.

Her Uncle Jim was at the back side of the pasture and had just headed the tractor toward her. She ran toward him waving her arm to get his attention. When he was about fifty yards away, he slowed and she heard him shut down the bush hog to avoid throwing dangerous broken pieces of trees or rocks at her as he pulled alongside. She quickly stepped up onto the tractor beside him and sat on the fender for the short trip to the truck.

Her Uncle Jim shared her father's blue eyes and tall, thin frame, but his curly brown hair, so different from her father's thick and graying straight hair, guaranteed that one would never be mistaken for the other. Rebecca leapt down from the tractor as soon as it stopped and introduced Olivia to her Uncle Jim. She shot her father a questioning look as they greeted each other, wondering what he had said while she was gone but he smiled innocently at her, worrying her even more.

The men were hungry and were glad to get the sandwiches and tea. "What are you girls up to this afternoon?" Willie asked, between bites of chicken salad. He tapped his index finger on the bill of Rebecca's cap. "You aren't planning on going deer hunting, are you?"

"No, just showing Olivia around some," Rebecca replied. "The caps were Mom's idea."

"Showing her the highlights of the big city of Springtown, Bec?" he said, jokingly.

"I thought about leaving the car here for a few minutes and walking over to show her Peacock Cemetery. It wouldn't be a full tour of town if I didn't show her our haunted graveyard, would it?"

The men both laughed at this, then spent the next few minutes trying to outdo each other with ghost stories they had heard associated with Peacock Cemetery. Rebecca had heard the stories all her life and didn't believe a word of them. Olivia seemed interested but Rebecca wasn't sure if she actually believed them or just enjoyed listening to their storytelling. If there was one thing her dad's family was good at, it would be telling a tall tale. She had learned years ago to look for a certain twinkle in the eye that none of them could disguise when they were getting windy. She could see both sets of blue eyes twinkling that afternoon.

Finally they finished their sandwiches and handed the bag and empty tea jug to Rebecca. Rebecca remembered to remind her dad about the early supper then she and Olivia headed back to the Buick to stow remnants of lunch. Rebecca pointed to a grove of trees across the field on the opposite side of Uncle Jim's house. "Peacock Cemetery is just beyond that stand of trees there. Are you up to walking a little more?"

"Sure," Olivia said. "Especially if it means going to a haunted graveyard." She laughed as she said this then continued in a more serious tone. "All those stories about people seeing a woman wandering the area looking for her lost baby really makes you wonder, though. Who knows what might have happened a century ago?"

Rebecca held the middle two wires apart so Olivia could step through the fence into the pasture. She showed Olivia how to hold the top wire up as she pushed down the second wire and also stepped through. On the way across the pasture, Rebecca explained, "Well, I'm not really sure I believe all those ghost stories. Some people say it's haunted but people say lots of things I don't necessarily believe. Dad and Uncle Jim are a couple of storytellers, too. I definitely take every story they tell with a grain of salt."

"I noticed how much they enjoyed it," Olivia noted. "If they're having that much fun with the telling of it, it makes you wonder how much they embellish it."

"Probably quite a bit, knowing those two," Rebecca admitted. "I wanted you to see Peacock Cemetery for a different reason, though."

Now she really had Olivia's interest. "I'm not sure what could be more interesting in a cemetery than a ghost but I'm all ears," she said.

"You don't look all ears," Rebecca joked then noticed as she said it that, no, Olivia definitely did NOT look all ears. She actually looked all curves and Rebecca appreciated the smooth rounding of her hips and breasts, so different from her own thin, lanky frame.

Rebecca hadn't noticed she had stopped walking while she appraised Olivia from head to toe until Olivia broke the spell and said, "I'm glad you noticed." Then she smiled that funny little smile and resumed walking toward the cemetery, leaving Rebecca to try to stem the hot blush which had rushed to her cheeks.

What is going on with me? When did I start cruising girls?

As she caught up to Olivia again, Rebecca found it difficult to look at her, instead looking everywhere else. She heard Olivia chuckle slightly and felt the blush start again. Finally, she was able to restore enough control to finish her original thoughts on the cemetery.

"The research I've been doing at the Genealogical Society and library is because of something I saw at Peacock Cemetery."

They had arrived at the old fence surrounding the cemetery and Rebecca opened the rickety gate and bowed slightly to usher Olivia through. Rebecca led her cautiously through the weeds until they stood before Mary Farthing's headstone. She told her about the newly overturned dirt she had found in front of the headstone two weeks previous. The dirt had packed again due to recent rains but no grass grew there yet, so she could easily see where the digging had occurred.

"I know this isn't as interesting or as important as your mystery," she said. "But nothing out of the ordinary ever happens around here so something like this seemed like a big deal to me."

"I think it's very interesting," Olivia countered. "Have you thought about digging down to see what's there?"

"No!" Rebecca almost shouted. "I don't know what part of that bothers me more, digging over someone's grave, or whatever it is we might find. Besides, Dad always said to be careful around old graves, there's a chance they could fall in if you walk over them."

"Okay, okay," Olivia laughed, putting her hand on Rebecca's arm to calm her down. "We don't have to dig. I'm sure there's more than one way to figure it out. What have you found out so far?"

Rebecca told her how Mary had moved to St. Louis several years before she died and of the secrecy surrounding her death. She hadn't been able to find any relatives in the area despite all her research. They looked closely at the other markers in the cemetery but garnered no new clues.

"Why does your dad think you would fall in a grave if you walk over it?" Olivia asked, stepping carefully around where she thought each coffin would be buried.

"They used to not put those concrete vaults in the ground to put the coffins into so over the years the wooden coffins would rot and the ground would settle and become soft at the top. I guess people would sink down into the dirt some if they walked over one in that condition. I've never seen it happen but I've always been told about it," Rebecca explained.

"Do you spend a lot of time in cemeteries then?" Olivia teased.

"Well, actually, more than you might think. In the summer, about once a month, Dad and I mow the family cemetery on the other side of town. Every Memorial Day, we have a family picnic at the old log church at the family cemetery grounds and about a month before that we have a work day and different members of the extended family show up to do upkeep on the old church and keep things repaired. I've also been to probably twenty or more funerals in my life."

"You've got to be kidding—twenty funerals?"

"Yeah, at least. I don't know, maybe more. I didn't really keep count, you know." Rebecca was surprised by Olivia's reaction. "Does that seem strange to you?"

"Yes," Olivia answered definitively. "I have been to a total of three funerals and I don't think I've ever known anyone our age who has been to nearly as many as you. Is this a secret hobby of yours or something? Is there some strange morbid side to you I need to know about?"

Rebecca laughed. "It's really not that unusual around here. Everyone in a small town knows everyone else. So every time anyone dies, almost the whole community either goes to the visitation, the funeral, the cemetery, or some combination of the three. Everyone stands around and visits with everyone else and if the deceased is from a large family like my dad's, it can be like a family reunion, especially when we all get together for the dinner afterward." Rebecca realized it was probably hard for someone from a big city with a scattered family to comprehend the local culture surrounding funerals.

"That sounds nice, in a way. I mean, if you could call a funeral nice, that is. It sounds like everyone kind of sticks together to get through the grief. That sure beats trying to handle it alone. I remember when my Gran died. I was about ten and I felt so isolated. Everyone sat quietly like they were afraid to talk. After the memorial service ended, everyone just went home like nothing had happened. Nobody talked about anything and I remember how confusing it was to me."

"That sounds like it must have been hard on you, just being a kid and all."

"I think I'd like your way a lot better."

Rebecca remembered Grandma's explanation about the circumstances around Mary Farthing's funeral. "Grandma said there was a lot of secrecy surrounding Mary's death. She died in the city and they brought her back to bury her close to their home. I got the feeling it wasn't a typical funeral for this area, either. I wonder why?"

"Maybe it's been Mary's ghost everyone has seen all of these years and the ghost did the digging," Olivia suggested in a teasing manner, changing the tone of their conversation.

"I think that's highly unlikely," Rebecca responded in a manner indicating her doubt in the presence of ghosts.

As they were leaving, Olivia asked, "Where does this little road go?"

"Oh, there's an old farmhouse up there." Rebecca had a sudden thought. "Do you still have that picture with you, Olivia?"

"Sure, here in my coat pocket," she said, pulling it out quickly.

Rebecca was already several steps ahead of her, hurrying up the small road. As she rounded a small bend to the abandoned, ramshackle farmhouse she eagerly turned and took the picture from Olivia. "I thought I recognized that house. This is it, I'm sure of it. This house used to look like that house in the picture."

At first, Olivia looked at the decaying building doubtfully. The roof had partially collapsed into the second story and the porch roof curved down like a grotesque clown smile between the first and second stories. Some of the rusted tin from the roof lay scattered across the yard, and the faded plywood that had once boarded all the windows had been removed in places, probably by vandals. She had a hard time imagining the house as it must have once appeared. After studying the picture again, however, she became as convinced as Rebecca. The windows were in all the right places, the general outline was the same.

Olivia grabbed Rebecca in a quick hug and jumped up and down with her. "You did it, Bec! You found the house!"

Suddenly both stopped moving, straining to hear a distant sound. From back around the bend came a sound of women laughing. "Did you hear that?" Olivia asked.

"Yeah, come on." Rebecca grabbed her hand and they dashed back along the route they had just taken. When they rounded the bend, they saw no evidence that anyone was there or had been there.

After looking around for a few more minutes, Rebecca walked back into the cemetery to look at Mary's headstone. She said, "I think I did more than find the house, Olivia. You know, the Farthings lived in that house when the picture was taken. I've seen copies of the deeds. I may have found MJ for you."

"Wow. I get it. You think MJ was Mary J. Farthing." Olivia had walked up behind her to consider the stone again and looked and sounded shocked that they had linked so many things together. "So, who was Ralph?"

"I'm not sure." Rebecca laughed. "You expect me to figure everything out for you? Do I look like Sherlock Holmes or something?"

Olivia donned a serious face and studied Rebecca from head to toe, causing Rebecca to blush hotly. "I would choose *something* to answer that question, and I don't believe you are all ears, either." She smiled that funny smile, turned before Rebecca could gather herself to respond, and headed back through the pasture toward Uncle Jim's house.

Rebecca followed, not hurrying to catch up immediately but letting her thoughts catch up with all the light flirting that had taken place so far. She decided she was okay with the direction things were heading so she picked up her pace to finish walking quietly beside Olivia.

On the drive back to Rebecca's house, they decided to look through their research again to see if they could find a link between MJ, Jane, or Ralph. They chose to combine their mysteries as one and the mood stayed light as they speculated wildly about how they could be linked. Olivia joked about getting a shovel and coming back to the graveyard at midnight. Rebecca told her she was crazy and if she fell into an old grave or was pushed into one by a ghost, it would serve her right. They entered Rebecca's house still laughing and teasing each other.

"I didn't realize your father and Uncle Jim were that amusing," her mother chimed in, which added to the girls' laughter. "And thank you for wearing your caps."

This only made them laugh more. As soon as they were able to control their giggles, they filled her in on the events of the afternoon. They both brought their notebooks to the table and looked through them as Rebecca's mother prepared supper. They had offered to help but she had shooed them away, telling them to work on their mystery instead. Although they were disappointed to not discover more clues in their papers, they still considered the afternoon a wonderful success.

CHAPTER SEVEN

Supper went quickly and Rebecca's parents asked Olivia questions about her experiences growing up on and around army bases. She also explained more about her family in St. Louis.

"My great-grandma was Jane Smith. We always called her Gran. She was the oldest child from a large family, they're all dead now. She died several years ago, at the age of ninety-nine. Smith was her maiden name, I guess she must have changed it back to Smith when my great-grandfather died. No one would ever talk about him, so I don't even know what his name was. The Smiths were an influential family in the city at that time. One of Gran's brothers was a banker, one was a doctor, her father was a judge. Gran lived with her parents while she raised my grandmother. Grandmama was her only child."

"Did you ever live with your Gran or Grandmama?" Beth asked.

"When we were little and my dad would deploy, Mom would move us, my two older brothers and me, to stay with one of Gran's younger brothers or sisters. They were all pretty old then, so we would have to play quietly and be on our best behavior. We were always glad when he was stationed stateside. Gran lived with Grandmama then. I don't know why but we never stayed with them."

"Sounds like you had to grow up pretty quick," Beth observed.

"I guess," Olivia said. "But it was okay. I mean, Mom and Dad had to sacrifice too, when he went away. It was kind of like that was our part. We were a team."

Rebecca and Olivia offered to clean up the kitchen after the meal, allowing Rebecca's parents to shower and change clothes to attend the visitation in Rockford.

"Girls, have a good evening," Rebecca's mother said as they left. "Olivia, make yourself at home. We should be back around nine or so."

"Bye," they said in unison as they put the last of the dishes back into the cabinets.

Rebecca suddenly realized she was alone with Olivia and the nervousness she had been fighting all day returned in a flash. "So, would you like to watch some TV or a movie?" she offered in a somewhat croaky voice.

Olivia shot her a strange look but followed her silently to the living room where Rebecca indicated the stacks of movies under the TV. Olivia knelt on the floor and flipped through the DVDs quickly. "Do you have any favorites?" she asked.

"I like some of the older ones, like *Beaches*, *Sleepless in Seattle* or *Fried Green Tomatoes*," Rebecca said. "But really, I'm not too picky."

"Let's watch *Fried Green Tomatoes*," Olivia said, picking out the DVD from the stack. "Do you have popcorn?"

"I can do better than that. I have popcorn *and* cherry Coke," Rebecca offered.

She hurried to the kitchen to put the popcorn in the microwave and returned with two tall glasses of cherry Coke, setting them on the coffee table. She showed Olivia how to get the movie started then returned to the kitchen for the popcorn. Just as the opening credits were rolling, she brought in a large bowl of popcorn and sat down next to Olivia on the sofa.

Rebecca was aware of her bad habit of stuffing herself with popcorn. She would catch herself shoving handful after handful into her mouth as if she were starving to death. Tonight, she was determined to control herself. After all, it was impolite and unattractive. *Uh-oh!* There went Rebecca's thoughts, out of control again. *So, now you're worried about whether you are attractive or not. What is that supposed to mean?*

Stop! She told herself, allowing a muffled sound to escape from the force of the command.

"Did you say something?" Olivia asked.

"Uh, no. I just belched. Must be the Coke. Excuse me." Rebecca was getting more flustered.

Olivia must have noticed her unease because she focused her attention on the movie, giving Rebecca time to collect herself. Finally, she relaxed and began to enjoy the movie, so much so that she barely noticed when Olivia moved the empty popcorn bowl from where it sat between them on the sofa and put it on the coffee table. Olivia shifted closer to her so their thighs touched lightly. Rebecca was surprised when the movie ended to find her arm along the back of the sofa behind Olivia's shoulders, and Olivia snuggled tightly against her side. She felt so comfortable, she didn't move as she used the remotes to turn off the DVD player and switch the TV to an all-music channel. She was trying hard to keep her mind quiet and to just enjoy this strange, warm new feeling of closeness.

"What do you think about the movie?" She had been so intent on staying relaxed that Olivia's voice almost made her jump.

"What do you mean?" Rebecca asked, suspecting Olivia had more than a general response in mind.

"Do you think they were just best friends or do you think they were lovers?" Olivia asked softly.

Rebecca had wondered that very thing every time she had seen the movie but had never been sure. "I don't know. But I'm not sure it really matters, because they obviously loved each other. They lived their lives together, as a family."

"Yeah, I guess you're right," Olivia said. She turned her head to look closely at Rebecca.

Their noses were only a few inches apart and Rebecca could feel Olivia's warm breath against her face. She sat motionless, and if the world was still turning, she was no longer a part of the rotation. Olivia smiled slowly then she gently leaned forward, closing the distance between them. When her lips touched Rebecca's, Rebecca thought she had never felt anything so soft, so hot and so smooth in her entire life. She felt like she was melting, starting at the lips. She nearly cried out when Olivia broke the contact.

Rebecca opened her eyes to see Olivia looking at her with that funny smile. "I hoped that was the reaction I was going to get," Olivia said quietly.

Rebecca answered by leaning toward her, seeking another kiss.

Rebecca's friends had teased her about being "Sweet 16," then "Sweet 17," then "Sweet 18." They had told her she didn't know what she was missing. She had told them they were crazy. Over the next several minutes, she made up for all that lost time, learning all she ever needed to know about the art of kissing. And although she had no one to compare her to, Olivia was about the best teacher anyone could ever hope to have. If kissing felt this good, she, not her friends, must have been crazy.

Rebecca's annoying thoughts had all been strangely silent during this time. She was too caught up in the feel of those fabulous lips then in the feel of Olivia's soft body pressed against hers, their breasts pressed together. Olivia stroked her hair, her face, her back. Rebecca ran her hands across the soft curves of Olivia's hips then pulled her closer, deepening the kiss, feeling like she wanted to pull Olivia into her own skin. Olivia moved one hand around and placed it between them, flat against

Rebecca's breastbone. She gently created a little space between them and slowly eased out of the kiss.

Rebecca felt flushed and a little disoriented. "Slow down a little, Bec," Olivia said softly. "It's okay. Remember where we are. Won't the parents be back in a little while?"

"Oh. Oh, yeah. Parents." Rebecca was having a little trouble organizing her thoughts. She turned to lean forward, elbows on her knees, and stared blindly at the TV.

"Are you okay?" Olivia asked, the concern obvious in her voice.

"Yeah," Rebecca said. "I'm the most okay I think I've ever been. I'm just not sure..." She trailed off into silence, unsure how to finish her thought.

"Not sure of what, exactly?" Olivia gently prodded. She reached to hold both of Rebecca's hands in her own as if she could feel what was going on inside of her.

"Um, lots of things. But I am sure of one thing," she said, sitting up straighter and turning to look again into Olivia's eyes. "I could become addicted to your kisses." She leaned in to kiss her again, demonstrating the truth of her words.

After several seconds of pure bliss, Rebecca was the one to back away. Olivia's words had remained in the back of her mind—*parents*. She was sure she wasn't ready to talk to them about making out with Olivia on the sofa in their living room. "As much as I am enjoying this, I think we have to stop for now," she said.

"I know," Olivia said, disappointment evident in her tone. "The parents."

They sat silently, smiling and holding hands as each drifted in the sea of each other's eyes for a few minutes. Then they both rose together, as if on cue, grabbed their empty Coke glasses and the popcorn bowl and headed to the kitchen. Rebecca returned to the living room to put away the movie and turn off the TV. When she entered the kitchen again, Olivia had refilled their glasses and sat down at the table. She was shuffling a deck of cards she'd found on the counter. Rebecca sat down opposite her and she dealt out a hand of rummy. "You do play rummy, don't you?" Olivia asked.

Rebecca nodded. "Don't tell Grandma."

"Don't tell Grandma what, about playing rummy, or about kissing you?"

"Uh, well, maybe both. I know what she'd say about us playing cards. She'd let us have an earful for that. The kissing, well, you never know what Grandma will say about some things."

"Oh." Olivia sounded relieved. "What about your parents?"

"Don't worry, they play cards," Rebecca teased. Then, more seriously, she added, "This is kind of new territory for me and for them. I mean, both my sisters married guys and gave my folks all the normal grief about dating." She suddenly felt a little shy, embarrassed to let Olivia know she had never dated, never even kissed anyone until that night. "I just never was interested in any of the guys at school."

"What about the girls?" Olivia asked. "Did you have a girlfriend?"

"No," she answered honestly. "I might as well 'fess up." She looked at the table as she continued. "I've never kissed anyone until tonight, guy or girl." She closed her eyes, unwilling to face the truth she had allowed to escape into the room.

Rebecca found the silence in the room deafening so she looked up from the table. Olivia had gotten up quietly from the table and had come around to her side. She squatted down and placed her hands on either side of Rebecca's face. "Thank you. Thank you for trusting me enough to let me be your first. I'm flattered." She kissed her briefly then leaned back on her heels to look into Rebecca's eyes again. "By the way, you do a pretty damned good job of kissing for someone with no experience. The guys and girls you went to school with don't know what they missed." She smiled and chuckled a little, then rose to her feet and returned to her chair.

Rebecca didn't know how to respond. She felt a little foolish but honored at the same time by Olivia's words. She just blushed hotly and smiled a sheepish smile.

Olivia asked her again, "So, what about your parents?"

"Mom and Dad would probably need a little time to get used to the idea but I think they would come around. They're already used to me doing things differently than either of my sisters. I don't think I'm ready to bring it up tonight, though," she added quickly.

"Don't worry, I won't kiss and tell," Olivia reassured her. "I do hope to get another opportunity to kiss more in the future, though."

"I think I could go along with that," Rebecca said softly.

* * *

Rebecca lost three hands of rummy in a row before her parents returned. She was usually very competitive with cards, but losing wasn't bothering her tonight. She was continually distracted by Olivia, by her eyes, her hair, her skin, her lips... She felt nearly weightless sitting in the chair, as if she were floating in a cloud of warmth and euphoria.

Rebecca's mother sat and talked to them for a few minutes before retiring for the night. She said nothing about Rebecca's distracted manner. She did seem surprised when she looked at the pad of paper where Olivia had been keeping score. "Rebecca, are you coming down with something?" she teased, putting a hand to her forehead. "I've never known you to lose three hands of rummy in a row."

Rebecca blushed a little but all she could come up with for a response was a drawn out, two-syllable, "Mo-om!"

"Okay," Beth said laughing. "I'll leave you alone. Don't stay up too late. Rebecca, show Olivia where the towels and washcloths are, if she wants a shower. I'll see you girls at breakfast."

"Goodnight, Mom." They were getting pretty good with responding in unison to her and their eyes met as they both smiled.

Two rounds later, Rebecca was starting to tire. It had been a day of high emotions and she was suddenly exhausted. She set Olivia up with towels for her shower then took one of her own as soon as she heard Olivia make her way to the guest bedroom. When she came back to her room, Olivia was sitting on the end of her bed dressed in an oversized T-shirt and boxer shorts, looking ridiculously adorable. Rebecca had been using a towel to dry her hair as she walked, ruffling it back and forth to absorb the moisture. At the sight of Olivia, she moved the towel quickly in front of her chest, suddenly self-conscious in her thin tank top and shorts. She pushed the door closed behind her, cautious that their voices might wake her parents.

"I just wanted to tell you good night," Olivia said. "Also, thank you for helping me investigate my mystery, or I should say *our* mystery. I really had a wonderful day, even before you let me kiss you."

"Good night," Rebecca said, sitting down beside her. "Thank you for helping me link my mystery to yours. I had a great day too, and I am so glad you decided to kiss me."

She kissed Olivia's soft, luscious lips, this time very aware of the presence of her parents two doors down the hall, and with enough restraint not to lose herself as completely as before.

Olivia moved away slowly then stood and walked away. She stopped at the door, turned and said softly, "Sweet dreams."

"Sweet dreams," Rebecca replied, equally softly.

Seconds later, she heard the door to the guest bedroom close quietly. For several minutes Rebecca sat on the edge of her bed staring at her image in the dresser mirror. She shook her head, not understanding what Olivia could see in her. Her hair was quickly drying in a whirlwind of directions. She noticed with dismay that her bare arms showed four markedly different tan lines. Her unremarkable features and nearly flat chest would never stop traffic.

Olivia, on the other hand, was the type that definitely could stop traffic. Rebecca closed her eyes and saw Olivia's smooth complexion complementing her sensuous lips and pert nose. Long eyelashes fluttered over enchanting green eyes. Her smile warmed Rebecca effortlessly. She fell back onto her bed without closing the door and was asleep in minutes, dreaming of soft, smooth lips and delightful curves.

CHAPTER EIGHT

Sunday morning, Rebecca awoke into a new world.

She felt different, like she finally fit into her own skin. All her struggles with change over the past several months, all the worry when her mind didn't seem to work like the minds of her friends—now she realized she simply hadn't given herself the opportunity to consider all of her options. The pathways she had considered just weren't right for her. The idea of making future plans with another woman was a possibility she hadn't thought about. But now that she was thinking about it, that type of future held endless potential.

Thinking back, she remembered learning from her friends what to look for in a guy, who was hot, who wasn't. But these weren't things she noticed unless prompted by her friends for her opinion. She had noticed Olivia's appearance immediately. She knew Olivia was a very attractive woman from the instant she set eyes on her in the dim light of the old courthouse. When Rebecca allowed it, Olivia could easily dominate her thoughts and daydreams. No one had ever done that before. She grinned foolishly as she realized that Olivia might even be worth all the drama which she had found so foolish and distasteful in her friends' lives.

She had heard the discussion many times about whether it was right or wrong to be gay. Some of her extended family belonged to fundamentalist churches and they said that gays would go to hell for their sins. She had never been quite sure she believed that because it seemed to her that God loved all his children, not just those who fit a certain pattern. This felt really right for her, like she had always been gay and just hadn't figured it out yet. So, if God made her this way, it must have been for a reason. And she didn't believe God made mistakes so he must have wanted her this way.

When she looked back over the past several years of her life, she realized that all those things she thought were strange about how she thought or acted while she was growing up weren't strange at all—if she were a lesbian. She felt like herself again, like she knew who she was again, and that had been missing for a long time, since childhood in fact.

"Morning, Mom," Rebecca said in the kitchen, reaching into the cupboard for a cup. She tried to sound nonchalant as she asked, "Seen anything of Olivia yet this morning?" Truthfully, Olivia had dominated her thoughts since before she had walked out her bedroom door. Rebecca poured her coffee and sat down next to her mother.

Her mother laid her paper down as if to get a better look at this new version of her daughter. "Actually, she must be an early riser. She's already had a cup of coffee and your father is giving her a grand tour of his machine shed. I'm not sure why, but she seems to find farm equipment interesting," she said with a wry smile.

"I think it's just all new to her, Mom." Rebecca knew her mother was teasing but still felt compelled to explain. "Dad loves a receptive audience so I'm sure they're enjoying themselves."

Her words were proven true seconds later when the two entered the back door, laughing and talking about his trials with his antique tractor. He had a newer tractor which Rebecca usually chose to use but his favorite, the Allis-Chalmers, was older than he was and seemed to be broken down more often than not. He had driven all over Missouri and called all over the country looking for parts in an attempt to keep it running. Rebecca never really understood what was so important about it, but it apparently was worth the effort to him.

She watched as they shook off the morning cold. Her father hung his lined flannel jacket on the coat rack and tossed his ball cap onto the top spike above it, then reached for Olivia's leather coat, hanging it up beside his. Rebecca watched Olivia turn away from him and scan the kitchen, settling quickly on where she sat at the table. Their eyes locked and everything else faded from Rebecca's mind.

"Biscuits are in the oven and now that sleepyhead here is awake, I'll get some eggs going," Rebecca's mother said, tousling Rebecca's hair as she walked around her. "Rebecca, get the eggs out for me and grab the bacon, too."

Rebecca was glad for the chores her mother directed her to do for the next several minutes. She had been instantly entranced when she had locked eyes with Olivia. The green of Olivia's eyes was brilliant this morning, no doubt enhanced by the emerald-green blouse she had chosen to wear. Rebecca had been unable to pull her eyes away until her mother intervened. She knew she would be unable to conceal how enamored she was if she continued to stare at her.

Breakfast was on the table quickly and Rebecca's father and Olivia kept up a discussion about farming in the rocky Ozark hills. Rebecca tried to keep her mind on the conversation instead of gaping at Olivia. As she listened, Rebecca realized that many facts of life she had taken for granted were not common knowledge to those outside of rural Missouri.

Finally, her mother broke in and asked if they were planning to do any research that day.

Rebecca answered first. "We figured out everyone in the picture but Ralph. I thought maybe Grandma might know something more. If we hurry, we might be able to catch her before she goes to church this morning. Is it okay with you,

Mom? We can help clean up the kitchen when we get back. I'll feed the cows then, too."

"You two run along and do your detective work," her mother insisted. "I can always work you harder another day to make up the difference," she teased Rebecca.

"Thanks, Mom," Rebecca said, giving her a quick hug. She hurried down the hall after Olivia, grabbing her notebook and jacket along the way.

In the front seat of the Buick, caught up in the mystery again, Rebecca was surprised when Olivia reached over to hold her hand. She maneuvered the Buick around potholes in the gravel road with one hand while squeezing Olivia's hand with the other. *It feels really good to just touch her*, Rebecca thought, and she smiled as she weaved the old car along.

A comfortable silence ensued throughout the short trip, with both lost in her own thoughts yet still linked through their hands. They exchanged a long, warm look after Rebecca stopped the car in front of Grandma's house. "We're here," she stated the obvious, at a loss for meaningful words, breaking the spell so quickly created between them.

They clambered out of the old Buick and walked side by side up to the door where Grandma was waiting for them. Rebecca wondered briefly if Grandma had noticed them sitting looking at each other for the long moment when they had arrived but there was no indication she had. They both received her trademark greeting and Olivia again responded to the warm bear hug with an equal squeeze for the affectionate woman. Rebecca suspected that unlike her own childhood, Olivia's had not been filled with these frequent displays of affection and she wasn't taking them for granted as Rebecca tended to do.

Olivia didn't waste time and jumped into an explanation about Mary Farthing and the old house by Peacock Cemetery. Grandma nodded. "I thought I knew that house. So, Mary Farthing is the MJ in your picture? Let me see it again."

Olivia pulled the picture out of her notebook and followed Grandma over to her recliner where she sat to study it. "Yes, I do believe that's Mary Farthing in the middle. I don't remember anyone calling her MJ, but it's possible. Ralph," she began, setting her finger on the lone male subject in the picture, "you know, I think the Farthings had a hired hand named Ralph. If it was him, he stayed with them for several years. I believe he lived in a small shack out behind their house. He took off several months before Mary died. I think the story was that he and Mr. Farthing got into a dispute over something and he just picked up and left town. I don't remember a last name, but Ralph seems right."

"Grandma, you are wonderful!" Olivia exclaimed, giving her another hug. "You've moved us one step closer to figuring this out. Did you ever meet Jane, the other woman in the photo? She was my great-grandmother."

"No, I didn't," she said. "Did she ever live around here?"

"I don't think so," Olivia said. "She was from St. Louis. MJ, or Mary, must have met her while she was living in St. Louis."

Grandma was looking at the picture with a slightly puzzled look. "Are you sure your great-grandmother is the one on the left? If I had to guess, I'd say you look more like the one in the middle. Maybe I'm wrong about which one is Mary."

"No, I have other pictures of Gran at home and I'm sure that's her," Olivia said, looking more closely at the picture as well. "But I see what you mean. I do resemble Mary some. Isn't that funny?" She slipped the picture back into her notebook.

"Grandma, do you believe in ghosts?" Olivia asked, going over to sit next to Rebecca on the sofa.

"I do. Rebecca's grandfather saw and heard a ghost right there at Peacock Cemetery."

"Really?" both girls responded to this. Rebecca hadn't heard this story before.

"Yes, he did. He was coming home with his mule and wagon from helping Mr. Johnson plow his fields. He stopped to open the gate by the Farthings so he could drive across the field to get home. It was dusk and he was trying to get home before all the light was gone. The old mule started spooking on him, he thought he heard a hoot owl off in the distance. He was able to get the mule calmed down and through the gate but he had to tie him to a tree while he closed the gate because he was still so skittish. Your grandfather came around that stand of trees and saw something moving over in the cemetery. Back then, there was a nice fence all around the cemetery. He thought it was a person, but whatever it was, it moved right through that fence like it wasn't even there. It was heading toward the old house, making that sound he thought was from the hoot owl. He gave the mule its head and let it tear out of there in the opposite direction with him and the wagon in tow, fast as it would go. He always said that was the fastest trip he ever made in a wagon across those fields. When he got home that evening, he was pale as a ghost. I was really worried because I thought something was wrong with him. But when he told me that story, I knew he believed every word of it."

"I know you were pretty young when he died, Rebecca, so you didn't know him very well. But your father and the rest of my children didn't get their storytelling skills from their father. They got them from my father. If your grandpa said that was what happened, then that was what happened."

"Now, why do you want to know if I believe in ghosts?"

"Well," Olivia began hesitantly, clearly not wanting to sound foolish.

Rebecca picked up the story for her. "Grandma, we heard something at Peacock Cemetery yesterday. It was right after we figured out about the house and the identity of MJ. We were still there by the house when we heard laughing coming from the cemetery. It sounded like two women laughing. We ran to the cemetery but couldn't see anyone around."

"Who knows, girls? Maybe it was laughter you heard. There are a lot of things in this world we just can't explain."

Grandma arose from her recliner and hugged Olivia, who was closest, then Rebecca. "Girls, I hate to rush you out the door but I think my ride to church is here." Grandma could see both of her driveways from her recliner and could also watch all the traffic that passed her house, so she never missed a thing.

They stepped out the door together and Rebecca introduced Olivia to her Aunt Sally, who had walked up to the porch to see what was keeping her mother. As they headed for the Buick, Rebecca and Olivia both had an extra spring in their step, full of excitement about their discoveries.

* * *

In a few minutes, they were back at Rebecca's house. Before they could look through their notes, Rebecca knew she had to feed the cattle. She brought out her notebook, set it on the kitchen table and encouraged Olivia to start without her. Then she headed to the front door where her work coat and bib overalls were hanging in the hall closet. She had stepped into her bibs and was pulling them up to fasten the straps when Olivia walked up behind her.

"Can I come along to help?" she asked.

"Sure," Rebecca said, pleased by her offer. None of her friends had ever shared her interest in livestock or farming. She looked down at the overalls she was wearing and realized she would need to find something to keep Olivia from getting too cold out on the tractor. "Mom, can Olivia borrow your overalls?" she yelled into the kitchen.

Beth appeared behind the girls and dug into the back of the closet, pulling out a worn pair of insulated overalls she kept handy for times when her husband needed her help with a new calf or a sick cow. "I think these will be a little loose but they'll certainly be better than going without," she said, holding up the overalls in front of Olivia's petite frame.

Olivia stepped into the overalls and Rebecca helped her untwist the straps so she could fasten them. Meanwhile, Beth had reached back into the closet and pulled out an old Carhartt coat for her to wear also. Soon they were both bundled up and heading out the door.

Olivia stood by as Rebecca got the tractor started and speared a bale. She opened the gate for her as she pulled the tractor close and Rebecca drove quickly through, then she leaped from the tractor to help Olivia get the gate closed without any cows escaping. Olivia nervously followed Rebecca back through the herd toward the tractor, clearly amazed at the confidence Rebecca showed as she pushed the cattle out of their way, talking to them as if they understood every word she said. She climbed up onto the tractor again and reached a hand down to help Olivia up. Olivia sat on the fender Rebecca patted and held tightly to a handle beside her with one hand and Rebecca's shoulder with the other.

"It's okay." Rebecca could feel by Olivia's tight grip on her shoulder that Olivia was on edge and tried to reassure her. "I promise I won't throw you off." She smiled at Olivia and saw a nervous smile cross Olivia's face at her words. She eased off the clutch and the tractor started forward slowly. Rebecca knew the cows were probably wondering why she was going so slowly but she didn't want Olivia to be afraid of riding with her as she followed her normal routine. When she hopped down from the tractor to remove the netting from the bale, Olivia started to step down, also.

"Why don't you stay up there? I'll be right back," Rebecca said.

Olivia sat down in the tractor seat and watched while Rebecca moved around the cattle, confident in her movements yet careful to be safe. Rebecca shoved the netting into a corner beside the seat then pulled herself up onto the tractor again. She sat down on the fender before Olivia had a chance to move from the seat.

"Okay, driver, let's unroll this bale!"

Olivia didn't look very eager to try driving the big machine, but Rebecca smiled encouragingly so she acquiesced. "What do I do?"

Rebecca led her patiently through the steps of moving the tractor forward, then showed her how to lower the hay bale to remove it from the spike. She guided Olivia as she turned the front of the tractor toward the bale and lowered the loader bucket to nudge it, causing the round bale to unroll. By the time she arrived back at the gate, she was still feeling pretty uncertain about her skills but Rebecca had pronounced her a pro. Olivia stepped down from the tractor after bringing it to a stop, bringing an end to her first tractor-driving lesson. She opened the gate for Rebecca to move the tractor through. After parking by the bales, Rebecca quickly walked over beside Olivia at the gate. They looked out across the pasture at the cows enjoying the hay.

"You really love working with them, don't you?" Olivia asked.

"Yeah, I guess I do. I like doing outside stuff and I love animals," she admitted.

"Maybe you should consider a career that involves working with them," Olivia suggested.

"Yeah, maybe," Rebecca answered noncommittally.

As if sensing her unwillingness to discuss career plans, Olivia changed the topic. "That was great. I can't believe I drove a tractor."

"You did pretty well for a rookie," Rebecca allowed. "Let's go to the house and look at our notes now."

After removing their work coats and overalls, they headed to the kitchen and sat down around the table with their notebooks spread out in front of them. As they reviewed their notes again, Olivia asked, "Census records? Do you have any notes about census records for the Farthings? Maybe they listed Ralph on their census in nineteen-thirty."

"I didn't get to that book," Rebecca confessed, thinking about their evening with the Genealogical Society. "But maybe I can reach one of the officers of the group this week and look at their records again. I don't think I could stand to wait until their next meeting."

Olivia agreed. "If you can take care of that I'll see what I can find out from Uncle Steve. He likes to talk and sometimes I can get him to tell me things he doesn't mean to. If I play him right, maybe he'll slip up," she laughed. "Does that sound like a plan, detective?"

Rebecca grinned and replied, "Sounds good to me, inspector."

Their eyes met and they grew quiet, each thinking what neither had said. Plans were easier to make for their investigations than they were for getting to see each other again. Thanksgiving was a week and a half away and family commitments couldn't be broken. They both had studying and classes, with end of semester less than a month away. And the more than two-hour drive between them didn't make things easier.

Rebecca drew up her schedule for the next few weeks on a piece of notebook paper. When Olivia saw what she was doing, she quickly did the same. They exchanged papers and Rebecca brightened when she noticed an opening in common.

"What are you doing next Saturday evening?" she asked, with a shy smile.

"Depends on what you have in mind," Olivia replied, lifting one eyebrow and smiling back at her.

"I could probably get the parents to let me meet you halfway if you want to meet for dinner," she suggested. "A couple of towns in that general area have a theater, if you want to catch a show."

"Are you asking me on a date?" Olivia teased quietly, aware of Rebecca's mother's presence in the next room.

"Yes," Rebecca responded quickly and with conviction.

"Then the answer is yes, I would love that."

Rebecca thought she would burst from the warmth that flooded her when she heard Olivia's response and the muscles in her stomach clenched when she saw that funny smile cross her face again.

They gathered their papers together and finalized their plans. Rebecca helped Olivia carry her things to her car. "What time do you have to leave?" she asked, not really wanting to hear the answer.

"I probably need to hit the road in about an hour." Olivia didn't sound any more eager to leave than Rebecca was for her to go.

"Let's go for a walk and we'll come back for a sandwich before you go," Rebecca suggested.

"Do you think it's safe with the deer hunters around?"

"It should be. Everyone lets Dad know before they hunt on us and with the leaves already fallen from the trees we can see a hunter in his orange for a mile," Rebecca reassured her.

"Why don't we take the sandwiches with us, like a picnic?" Olivia said.

"It's a little cold for a picnic, but that's okay with me if that's what you want to do," Rebecca agreed. "I guess we could wear overalls again."

"Maybe I can think of some way to keep you warm," Olivia suggested as she turned to head back into the house.

Rebecca blushed and was unable to move for a couple of seconds. She ran to catch up and caught the door just before it closed behind Olivia.

Ten minutes later, with a Thermos filled with steaming hot coffee and ham sandwiches, chips, and two cups placed in a bag, they donned their insulated bib overalls again, placed their blaze-orange caps on, and added blaze-orange vests at Beth's insistence. They carried their meal across the back pasture, crossed the fence to the adjoining pasture and continued over the hill to the back corner of the property. As they walked, they kept their eyes out for hunters, easily identifiable in the bright orange, but they neither saw nor heard any and were glad for the privacy.

Rebecca knew this corner was the most secluded part of the farm. She had told her father that she wanted a house there some day, away from the rest of the world.

"It's beautiful back here," Olivia said. "Rugged and so private, like the rest of the world has disappeared."

"That's why I like it," Rebecca said. She showed Olivia a tree to set their food under then she grabbed her hand and led her around her dream house, showing her the view out her imaginary front window and sitting beside her on her illusion of a porch.

Finally, Olivia looked at her watch. "We had better eat then head back."

They ate quickly and in silence, watching a squirrel scamper around from tree to tree in the draw below them, making sounds like a much larger animal as it crashed through the leaves. They heard distant shots from time to time but Rebecca assured

Olivia they were miles away, with the sound traveling along the draws and hollers around them.

She gave Olivia a quick vocabulary lesson about the geography of the area. A *ridge* was easily understood to be a long, high run of land. A *holler* was the converse, a low place between ridges, but wide enough to form a *bottom*. A *draw* was a more narrow cut between ridges, sloping down steeply but not opening into a bottom. Olivia was amused to learn the new meanings, not realizing that only two hours away from her apartment in the city, people spoke a different language.

They placed the remaining chips and their cups into the bag, gathered their trash and stood, sweeping the dried grass and leaves from their clothing. Rebecca looked up from brushing off the back of her overalls to find Olivia facing her about a foot away. In all her bundled glory, she resembled an orange Michelin man. The cap turned backward over her riotous curls made her adorable. "I'm glad you brought me here," she said as she stepped forward and rested her hands on Rebecca's shoulders. Rebecca saw the fire in Olivia's beautiful green eyes as she drew her closer until their warm lips touched. Rebecca closed her eyes, overwhelmed by the feeling of Olivia's lips gently moving against her own. Rebecca stepped in and pulled Olivia as close to her as their padded bodies would allow. The kiss became more urgent as their passion grew, and Rebecca's knees began to weaken when Olivia's tongue touched hers and the kiss deepened. When she knew she couldn't remain standing for another second, she broke away from the kiss. Olivia helped her balance as she took a sudden step to stay upright.

"Maybe it's safer if I'm sitting down when you do that," Rebecca said, sounding a little breathless.

"It does seem to produce a powerful reaction when we kiss, doesn't it?" Olivia smiled. "I thought when I met you that you were something special but I had no idea you would be able to turn my world upside down with a kiss." She had been slowly moving Rebecca backward as she spoke. "One more, before I go?" she asked. She pressed Rebecca back against the massive oak tree they had picnicked under, pinning her against it with her soft body. Not waiting for a response, Olivia captured Rebecca's lips again.

Rebecca had nowhere to go with the tree behind her but she couldn't have pulled away this time if she had wanted to. She felt everything else slip away as she became lost in Olivia, her lips, her hands caressing her face, then under her jacket along her sides and her back, under the layer of overalls, her hips pressing urgently against her as they kissed. A pressure was building deep within her and she knew she wanted to get closer, closer than she could through this winter clothing. The tree impeded her efforts to shrug out of her jacket and much too soon, she felt Olivia begin to ease away. Rebecca chased after her lips until Olivia placed a hand flat against her chest and gently pressed to still her.

After a few seconds, Rebecca felt the world begin to come back into focus around her. She felt a smile slowly spread across her face and she saw Olivia's eyes gradually lose their fire, changing to banked embers. Rebecca wasn't sure she was ready for whatever could follow that kiss, at least not out in the cold November air in the back corner of the pasture. She wasn't even sure a body could stand to experience something beyond the feelings that filled her from that kiss. She already felt like she had been close to shattering. Although she was a little frightened to imagine feeling more, at the same time her body yearned for her to push forward. But the few seconds of separation had given her brain the upper hand so she broke the spell their bodies had created together and spoke softly to Olivia. "I guess we'd better go now...while I'm still able to walk." She added the last part as she noticed her legs beginning to function again, helping the tree and Olivia support her weight.

Olivia stepped back slowly until she had released her completely. Retrieving the bag and Thermos, she held both in one hand as she grabbed Rebecca's hand with the other. She led her down the path they had taken until Rebecca quickly came into step beside her. They exchanged smiles and smoldering looks until they neared Rebecca's house. Then they dropped hands to climb the final fence and put a little more space between their paths as they crossed the yard to the back door.

Rebecca hoped she had herself under control as they walked into the kitchen where her mother sat at her favorite spot, this time reading the Sunday edition of the St. Louis paper.

"How was your picnic?" she asked. "It looks like that cold air chapped your faces a little, your cheeks are certainly red," she noted, looking around the paper at the two girls.

"We're fine," Rebecca said, a little abruptly. "I'm going to walk Olivia out to her car. She's got to get back and study some this evening," she added, trying to distract her mother's attention from their appearance. If her expression looked anything like Olivia's, she realized, her mother must really be wondering what they'd been up to. Olivia's dreamy expression, the starry eyes and disheveled cap and coat made a curious picture. Rebecca led her to the hall closet and they quickly removed their vests, caps and overalls and Olivia put on her own coat.

"Good-bye, Mom," Olivia said, stepping around the table to give her a hug. "Thank you for letting me stay."

"Olivia, you are always welcome," she replied sincerely.

At the door, Rebecca turned. "Oh, yeah, Mom. Olivia and I talked about meeting next Saturday between here and the city for dinner and maybe a show." When her mother raised an eyebrow, she continued quickly, "To go over any clues we might discover this week. The Buick has been running good, my studies are caught up and I wouldn't be driving all the way in to the city. You know I'll be careful."

"We have to let you stretch your wings sometime," her mother admitted. "Let me talk to your father, he worries about you getting too far from home. I don't know how he's going to survive when you go away to finish college."

"Thanks, Mom." Rebecca knew her mother would get her father to agree. She also knew her mother was just as upset at the prospect of her moving away as her father was, although she tried not to let on.

She ushered Olivia out of the house quickly, wanting to escape any further scrutiny from her mother.

The quick hug good-bye at the car was mutual, each cautious not to push through the other's thin veneer of self-control.

"Call me," Rebecca said, holding her phone up to Olivia. Olivia smiled and nodded, then drove away.

Rebecca was left standing by the road, feeling alone in a way she had never felt before, not here, not surrounded by a community full of relatives and friends. She watched Olivia's car weaving its way around the potholes in the road until it disappeared over a small rise.

CHAPTER NINE

For the remainder of the day, Rebecca found things to keep herself busy, out of the sight of her mother for the most part. She studied in her room, trying to get ahead on any subject possible to reduce her study load for the following weekend. Olivia had sent her a quick text three hours after she left, letting her know she had made it back to St. Louis safely. That reminded Rebecca that she had promised Olivia she would try to find the census records. She retrieved the phone book from the living room and found the number of the Genealogical Society president. A quick call was all it took to set up a time to look at their records. Thursday at 6:30 p.m., she would meet him at the old courthouse. She texted the information to Olivia, who responded with, *Great work, Sherlock!* This only reminded her of Olivia's flirting at the cemetery and she blushed slightly as she remembered how it had made her feel.

Knowing she could spend hours talking to Olivia on the phone, Rebecca made herself wait until 9:00 p.m. each evening that week before calling. They had decided she should be the one to call so her parents wouldn't question Olivia calling so much. They spoke of their day at school, their favorite classes, their least favorite professors, Olivia's cat, Pooh, and more. Each wanted to know everything about the other and even the mundane things sounded exciting.

Thursday evening, after going to the old courthouse, Rebecca didn't think the clock would ever get to nine so she could call Olivia with her news. The clock in the kitchen was still chiming the hour as she hit speeddial.

"Dunlop," she blurted out as soon as Olivia answered. "Ralph Dunlop."

"Oooh!" Olivia squealed into the phone. "You found another piece of the puzzle!"

"I found more than that," Rebecca added excitedly. "Mr. Johnson, the president of the Genealogical Society, heard me say the name when I found it. He said he used to know a Ralph Dunlop. He lived about fifty miles north of Springtown and was kind of a hermit. You know, he lived by himself in an old shack out in the country. He worked as a farmhand most of his life, according to Mr. Johnson."

"Wow, you are a great detective!" Olivia sounded gratifyingly surprised at how much Rebecca had learned. "Did he know where Ralph lives now?"

"No, he's not even sure he's alive," Rebecca said. "He said the old shack burned down about ten years ago and the few acres it sat on are all grown over with brush now."

Olivia didn't respond immediately, so Rebecca continued. "He lived in the next county north of us, so we can go to the courthouse there and look through their records." With disappointment she added, "But that would probably have to wait until the semester ends. I can't afford to miss any more classes."

"I know what you mean," agreed Olivia. "I'm struggling to keep my mind on classes now. Let's not worry about going there yet, maybe I'll get more information when I talk to Uncle Steve next week. He'll be at Grandmama's for Thanksgiving dinner."

They spent the next half hour sharing stories of previous Thanksgivings with their families. Rebecca's memories were of a small house overflowing with aunts, uncles and cousins, with people sitting on the beds and the furniture and the floors throughout the house while they ate, until there wasn't a place left in anybody to put another bite. Olivia's memories contrasted sharply with hers: a large house, a large dining room table and the largest gathering she could ever remember numbering fifteen. Rebecca remembered noise, laughing, talking and joking, and everyone bringing food and preparing even more food when they arrived. Olivia remembered polite conversations around a meal prepared by others, followed by the men gathering in the den, the women in the formal living room and the children expected to play quietly in the nursery or read in the library.

Finally, they said their good nights, each knowing she had to hang up to finish studying for the following day.

* * *

Saturday morning after breakfast, Rebecca's father left to help his brother work on some equipment. Rebecca washed the breakfast dishes for her mother.

"I haven't seen much of you this week," her mother commented from behind her paper.

"School's kept me pretty busy," Rebecca said, concerned over which way the conversation might be headed.

"How's Olivia?" her mother asked, peering around the edge of her paper.

"Oh, uh, good, I guess," Rebecca stammered, staring out the window in front of her.

"That's good," her mother said. "Are you still meeting her this evening?"

"Yeah, we've got it all set up. I'm leaving at four but I probably won't be home until late," Rebecca said, returning to scrubbing the skillet. *Maybe she's going to let me off the hook.*

"Just be careful, especially driving home that late," she cautioned.

Rebecca had just started to relax when her mother continued. "I know you've been going through some changes lately, growing up, I guess. I also can see how much this friendship with Olivia means to you. Just know I'm here for you, regardless. I mean that, *regardless*." She emphasized the last word.

After a few seconds of silence, Rebecca answered quietly, still not looking at her mother, "You're right, Mom. I am going through some stuff but I think it's all for the good. I'm starting to understand myself a little more, you know, what makes me tick."

She paused a few seconds but her mother didn't respond, so she continued. "I know I usually talk to you when I have a problem but this isn't really a problem. It's more like I'm figuring out *me*. As soon as I know for sure what I've learned, I promise I'll talk to you about it."

Her mother had set her paper down on the table to listen to this explanation. Now she seemed to choose her words carefully as if cautious not to push her daughter beyond what she was willing to share and eager to keep their lines of communication open. "Rebecca, turn around for a minute, please."

Rebecca did as she was told and tried to keep eye contact as her mother continued. "After raising two other daughters, I thought you wouldn't offer any new challenges. However, I think I've had the least to offer you in some ways, to help you get through your teenage years. These past few months, you've been struggling to find your own way. That makes you more independent and stronger than your sisters. That also leaves me feeling helpless when I see you struggle. Just know, even though I may not know how to help you, I'll always love you and always be here for you. I believe you're going to find the path you were meant to follow."

Rebecca felt her eyes beginning to tear up and she hated crying. "Thanks, Mom. I love you, too. You give me just enough," she said. "Just enough advice, just enough support and just enough freedom for me to be me. I hope I never disappoint you with the choices I make," she added, thinking of Olivia.

Her mother held her gaze firmly with her own as she responded, "You have made no choices lately that have disappointed me." Then, she lifted her paper again and added in a teasing voice from behind it, ensuring Rebecca would know what she meant. "Oh, by the way, enjoy your date tonight with Olivia."

Rebecca knew she had intentionally used the word *date* from the way she emphasized it. She stared at her mother's paper. *How did she know?* Sometimes, she thought her mother was a mind reader. *What about Dad, what had she told him?* Rebecca didn't want to think about that yet.

She turned wordlessly and finished cleaning out the sink then wiped the counters and stove. Before she walked from the room, she reached around from behind and hugged her mother. She just got her bedroom door closed when the tears came, tears of confusion, tears of love for her mother and tears of relief that her mother knew how she felt about Olivia and wasn't disappointed in her.

"Suck it up, Bec," she whispered. After a few minutes, she pulled herself together then grabbed a textbook she needed to study. She started to sit on her bed to read like she had done all week, but changed her mind. She opened the door and walked back to the kitchen, choosing to sit at the table with her mother as they both read.

* * *

By two o'clock, Rebecca was starting to get ready. She remembered how she used to torment her sisters when they were getting ready for their dates. She had never understood what the big deal was. Did it really matter which way their hair was fixed, or whether they wore a pink blouse with frills or the white silk blouse? Now she felt a little foolish as she stood before her mirror trying to get her cowlick to cooperate. She wanted everything to be perfect.

Finally satisfied that at least her hair wasn't sticking up wildly, she looked closely at her reflection. Hair—passable, better than usual and no hat ring. Complexion—she didn't want to think about it. The new zit on her chin made her question whether she wanted to ask for her mother's help in making it disappear. June and Kate had tried for years to teach her the ins and outs of makeup but she had never wanted to learn. Now maybe she should reconsider.

Outfit—okay. She was pleased with the yellow shirt she wore unbuttoned over a black tank, the sleeves cuffed at mid-forearm. Her black jeans and a black pair of loafers completed the package, leaving her still comfortable yet looking classier than she did in her normal attire—jeans, sneakers and T-shirt or flannel shirt, depending on the weather. She fastened a leather cord necklace with a turquoise pendant around her neck and checked her image again.

"Damn zit!" she complained loudly. After looking at her chin for the hundredth time, she finally decided it wasn't going to disappear, nor was it going to become any less noticeable on its own.

"I wish your sisters were here to harass you," her mother teased as she applied concealer over the small blemish on Rebecca's chin. "You know you deserve it, right?" She finally pronounced her repair work complete and handed Rebecca a small mirror so she could see the finished product. "As long as you don't rub your chin on your shirt tail before you get there, you'll look fine," her mother teased.

As Rebecca headed out to the Buick, she passed her father on the front porch.

"You look great!" he said, sounding a little surprised as he scanned her from head to toe. "My little tomboy grew up when I wasn't looking," he teased a little wistfully.

"Thanks, Dad," she said sincerely. She gave him a quick hug. "I'll see you in the morning."

"Oh, that's right. You're going to meet Olivia. Have a good time and *be careful*," he stressed.

"You know I will," she said as she opened the car door to the Buick.

Rebecca gave her thoughts their freedom on the seventy-minute drive. It no longer seemed like a war being waged between her ears. Instead, it was a kaleidoscope of daydreams with Olivia in all of them. She was surprised at how quickly the time passed. Before she knew it, she was pulling into the parking lot of the steakhouse where they had agreed to meet.

Olivia's car sat at the side of the building and Rebecca parked in an empty spot beside it. She turned off the old Buick and pulled the key from the ignition, reached into the passenger seat to retrieve her wallet. About to open her door, she looked out her window. Her breath caught as she saw Olivia standing between the cars, waiting for her. *Damn, she looks good!* Her dark brown hair curled softly around her face and her sensuous red lips curved in a warm smile as her eyes met Rebecca's. Olivia made her pulse jump with just a look and Rebecca realized suddenly how relieved she was that it hadn't all been a dream. This was a real date—with one beautiful and sexy Olivia Harmon.

"Hi," Rebecca greeted Olivia as she stepped out of the car. "I got here early and you still beat me. Have you been waiting long?"

"I've just been here a minute," Olivia said. "I hope this isn't turning into a contest," she teased. "If so, I may have to set my watch ahead so I can keep an advantage over you."

They entered the restaurant laughing and joking. Rebecca could never remember afterward what she ordered or how it tasted. She knew she would always have good memories of the place, though. The meal flew by. Before they knew it, it was half an hour before the movie was due to start. They agreed to split the bill then headed out to the cars together.

"So, have you decided what show you're taking me to see?" Olivia had insisted if she chose the restaurant, then Rebecca must choose the movie.

"I had a couple of ideas but I wanted your input," she said. Olivia put a hand on her hip and began to protest, but Rebecca quickly interrupted. "Let me explain. There is a good movie showing, but there's also a state park about five miles out of town. The gates stay open until nine. I thought we could drive out and talk for a while. But if you'd rather see the movie, that's okay with me."

Olivia looked intrigued. "That sounds great to me," she said. "Can we take your car and leave mine here?" she asked.

Rebecca unlocked the Buick. A mile outside of town, Olivia unbuckled her seat belt and slid to the center of the bench seat, fastening the waist belt then snuggling in closer to Rebecca as she drove the dark highway. A few minutes later, Rebecca turned into the gate of the park. Her headlights illuminated the sign warning that the gate would close at nine. "Help me watch the time," she told Olivia.

"I'll set the alarm on my phone for eight-fifty," she said, quickly digging in her coat pocket for her phone.

"I knew you were a genius when I met you," Rebecca teased lightly.

"I knew you were hot when I met you," Olivia countered. In the dim light coming from the dashboard, she saw Rebecca blush deeply and she chuckled.

Rebecca drove the car to the end of the drive, stopping in the middle of the road at one point to allow deer to pass in front of the car. Olivia counted fourteen deer before they finished passing by and the herd walked slowly to the center of the deserted campground before bedding down. Rebecca slowly eased the car on past them, careful to not disturb them. A single light illuminated the parking lot at the end of the drive and Rebecca parked the car in a shadowy corner overlooking the river, which stretched out dark and forbidding before them.

Rebecca removed her seat belt so she could turn in the driver's seat to look at Olivia. She shook her head, still slightly amazed. "I have to keep reminding myself that this is real, that I'm really on a date with you," she explained. "I'm afraid I'll wake up and it'll all be a dream."

"Why?" Olivia sounded puzzled. "Why wouldn't it be real?"

"Because...because you're you and I'm me."

"What's that supposed to mean? Of course you're you and I'm me. Who else would we be?"

"I mean..." Rebecca was trying hard to explain but wasn't exactly sure what she was trying to say. "You're so beautiful, and I'm sure there are several women you know who would love to go out with you, yet here you are with me."

"I'm not sure about all of that," Olivia said modestly. "Besides, why wouldn't I want to be out with you? Have you looked in the mirror lately? If you were any hotter, Bec...your strong arms, that sexy hair that fights to do its own thing, just everything about you. You're real, not like so many people I know. You're not pretending to be something you're not. Do you know how rare that is?"

It seemed unbelievable to her that being Rebecca Wilcox could be considered desirable. All her life, she felt she had come up short of people's expectations for what she should look like, how she should dress and how she should act. She didn't chase after guys like her sisters and her girlfriends. She didn't wear dresses or makeup. She hadn't even played with dolls when she was a child, preferring to climb trees or jump out of the hayloft.

She looked at Olivia in wonder. "How did I find someone as special as you?"

"Just lucky, I guess," Olivia said with a wink. "So, tell me this. What's your plan now that you've found me?"

Her sudden question left Rebecca momentarily speechless. "Do you mean, what are my plans for this evening, or what are my plans for the future?" Rebecca asked, unsure how she would answer either question.

Olivia lifted her eyebrows. "This evening might be interesting, but first I want to know about the future. What do you want to do with your life, Bec?"

"I don't know. I never thought much beyond getting out of high school and getting into college. Mom's always nagging at me to figure it out, but I just don't know what I want to do."

"You showed me your dream house, remember?"

"Yeah. But I never thought about a time frame for it. Will I retire there? Will I build it when I get out of college? I just don't know."

"Do you want to have a farm?"

"Maybe. I like working with animals. I guess it's kind of like what you said about people. So many people pretend to be something they're not. People are confusing and hard to figure out. Animals are easy. They operate under pretty basic instincts for the most part and as long as you understand what motivates them, you know what they're going to do."

"Do *people* make you nervous, Bec?"

"Yeah, a little. Especially large crowds.

"Do you think you could ever live in the city?" Olivia asked.

"Sure. I thought I'd probably have to move somewhere to finish college and maybe even to work after college, depending on what I decide to major in. What about you, Olivia? What's the future hold for you?" Rebecca reached up and tucked a wayward curl behind Olivia's ear, smiling as it popped out again only seconds later.

"Well, I'm majoring in English literature. I haven't made up my mind for sure but I'm leaning toward teaching. I've always loved reading. If a kid enjoys reading, it can open up a whole world of possibilities. If I can share my love for books with even one child, I can help change the world." Olivia ducked her head. "I probably sound pretty crazy, don't I?"

Rebecca ran a finger along her jaw to her chin and tilted her head up until she could see her eyes. "I don't think you sound crazy. I think you sound pretty wonderful. I think you'd make a great teacher."

Olivia's pleasure at her words shone in her eyes and Rebecca nearly fell into them. She wanted to know more, though, so she reeled in the desire which had been simmering since she saw Olivia outside the car at the steakhouse. "Olivia, when did you know…when did you know you liked women?" Rebecca asked.

"I guess I knew for sure when I was seventeen. I wondered before that, probably since I was about fourteen or so, but then when I met Lacy, there was no denying it."

"Lacy?"

"Yeah. She was my first girlfriend. We were in the same grade in high school. We had just moved and the principal at our new high school assigned her to show me around to all my classes. There was this immediate connection, like we had known each other before but we hadn't. She had already come out to her family, but only her friends at school knew she was gay. Anyway, six months later her father deployed to Germany and he insisted the whole family go along. My parents offered to let her stay with us to finish high school but her father said no.

We wrote and Skyped for a while, but slowly we went on with our lives apart. I haven't heard from her in nine months."

"Did your parents know you were girlfriends?"

"Not at first. They found out the week before she left." Olivia's voice was flat, emotionless.

"How did they take it?" Rebecca asked, suddenly wary.

"Mom went ballistic. Dad just stopped talking to me for about a month. They finally came around but it was pretty bad for a while." The sadness of the past reflected in Olivia's eyes.

"Oh, Olivia. I'm sorry. That must have been awful."

"It wasn't great. But it's all in the past now. Let's talk about something else. Let's talk about you and me." Olivia forced a smile. "Rebecca, I may have figured out what I wanted a little before you. But, this has been different somehow, with you. It's like we connect at a different level." She looked directly into Rebecca's eyes, her own softly glowing in the filtered light from the distant parking lot light. "I've never known anyone who could melt me with a kiss the way you do. You must be a natural," she teased, smiling at the slight blush that crept into Rebecca's cheeks again.

Olivia placed a hand on either side of Rebecca's fiery cheeks and gently pulled their lips together, as if to prove her point. Several minutes later, Rebecca looked up and noticed the steamy windows. Like one of those crazy movies, she thought. Their coats became hindrances and entirely unnecessary in the increasingly warm front seat, so they removed them and tossed them into the back seat.

They sat smiling at each other for a few seconds then their lips met again. The intensity of the sensations that flooded through her left Rebecca breathless, teary-eyed, and feeling like she might explode. Hands and lips roamed over faces and necks. She thought she would pass out when Olivia reached up under her shirt, caressing at first then gently teasing her nipples. Rebecca was surprised at how her own hands burned as she did the same, sliding her hands first under the back of Olivia's blouse, marveling in the silkiness of her skin. Then she slid her hands slowly around the front to cup her breasts. Even through the thin laciness of her bra, she could feel the heat from her skin and feel the nipples harden under her touch.

She heard a deep moan and was surprised to realize she was making the sound, letting out some of the pressure building within her. Olivia pushed Rebecca back against the door and brought her knees up onto the seat so she could move over her. Seeking to get even closer, touch her even more, Rebecca slid down on the seat, pushing her leg up beneath Olivia. She reached around Olivia's hips and pulled her down tightly against her. The electric shocks emanating from her lips and her breasts traveled down to her very center and she found herself lifting her hips to press against Olivia more. Olivia shifted slightly and brought her thigh between Rebecca's legs, trapping her leg between her own thighs.

Rebecca had lost all thought of anything but Olivia, overcome with the onslaught of sensations Olivia was causing to course through her body. She began hearing a pattern of beats and wondered insanely if it was bells she was hearing. After several repetitions of the sound, she realized the sound was coming from a few feet to her right.

She struggled to return to her senses, trying to identify the sound, knowing it was important but unable to decide why. She moved her hands up to Olivia's waist, lifted her slightly to reduce the pressure against her and began to ease the kiss.

Feeling her withdraw physically and emotionally, Olivia gazed at her when their lips separated and Rebecca saw confusion and concern cross her face initially then suddenly, surprise, as she too realized what the sound was. She pulled her hands from beneath Rebecca's shirt and popped up onto her knees in the seat. Rebecca scooted herself back into a sitting position as Olivia reached into the back seat to search her coat pockets for her phone. Rebecca could not resist the temptation and reached up to trace the curve of Olivia's hips and buttocks as she knelt in front of her. Olivia laughed and slapped at her hand as she plopped back down in the seat beside her.

"Hey, that's not fair!" she yelped. Rebecca grabbed her and began tickling, starting a brief wrestling match full of laughter, each trying to out maneuver the other in the small space afforded by the car. They stopped, breathless and exhausted both from the tickling and the more intimate contact which had preceded it.

"We had better go," Rebecca said, feeling a sudden sense of urgency. "That gate will close in five minutes."

She started the car and they buckled in as she slowly drove the weaving path out of the park, watching closely for more deer. They pulled past a surprised park ranger at the gate where he was preparing to close the road for the night. "He'll probably wonder about us for a while," Rebecca noted. "Two young women alone in a dark, deserted park on a cold November night." Then she added after a glance in the rearview mirror, "With the rear windows still fogged up."

This sent Olivia into fits of laughter which Rebecca encouraged by coming up with possible scenarios for their escapade. When she pulled up beside Olivia's car in the nearly empty parking lot of the steakhouse, Olivia was holding her sides from laughing so hard.

"I love making you laugh," Rebecca said, looking more seriously across the car at her. Olivia had moved over closer to the car door when they had reentered the city limits, where the streets were well-lit and the traffic was heavier.

"I love it when you make me laugh," Olivia said in a suddenly serious voice. "As a matter of fact, there are a lot of things about you I love." She reached over and grabbed Rebecca's hand, then turned the palm up to trace the lines on it. Rebecca wasn't sure if Olivia knew she was sending electrical jolts from her palm to the very center of her being with each touch of her fingertip.

"I feel the same about you. These feelings I'm having are all pretty new to me, you know," she reminded Olivia. "But, Olivia, I think I may be falling head over heels for you."

Olivia looked thrilled initially, then a little concerned, then cautious as she stopped tracing her palm and grasped her hand firmly between hers instead. "I think what I'm feeling for you is different than anything I have felt before. I'm also feeling things that are new. But I don't want you to get ahead of yourself. Don't feel like you need to explain your feelings to me until you know for sure how you feel and what you want. If nothing else, I want us to always be honest with each other."

"I want that, too," Rebecca said. "I can't promise where this is going to lead, but I can promise honesty." She squeezed Olivia's hand in her own. "Thank you for a wonderful evening," she added.

"No, thank you for a wonderful evening," Olivia insisted. "What's next?" she asked. "When am I going to get to see you again?"

"I can't say for sure," Rebecca said. "But we can keep in touch and maybe our schedules will give us a break between now and the end of finals. By the way," she said and smiled. "You can call me now if you want. I forgot to tell you that my mother is an amateur psychic. She told me to enjoy my *date* with you."

"What?" Olivia's eyes flew open. "What else did she say?"

"You know, that she supports me and loves me and all that normal mom-talk," Rebecca said, trying to gloss over the emotional discussion she'd had with her mother.

Olivia looked down as she said, "You don't know how lucky you are to have the family you have. My mom blew a gasket when she caught me and Lacy kissing in my bedroom. She told me I could never tell Grandmama, that it would kill her. I believe it might, too, so only my parents and my brothers know."

Rebecca hadn't known that Olivia had to hide part of her life from her grandmother. She wished she could wipe away the hurt she saw on Olivia's face. "I guess you're right, I am pretty lucky," she agreed. "I'm sorry about your grandmama, though. Do you think she'll ever change?"

"I doubt it," Olivia said. "It would take something pretty big to make her change." She lifted her eyes to look at Rebecca again. "I'd better go before we both get too tired to drive. I'll call you tomorrow afternoon. Tell your parents I said hello." She looked uncertainly around the parking lot then leaned over and gave Rebecca a quick kiss good-bye.

Moments later Rebecca turned the Buick around and followed Olivia out of the parking lot and to the interstate highway. It was difficult to keep going instead of following

Olivia as she turned right to go east, but Rebecca gripped the steering wheel tightly, crossed the overpass, and turned west.

It was nearly eleven when she got home. The house was dark and she moved quietly down the hall to her bedroom. Her phone alert signaled a text message as she tossed her coat across the foot of the bed. It said, simply, *home. miss you.* She wasted no time replying with the same words.

She slept fitfully that night, trying to shut off the memory of Olivia's body pressed warmly against her own. She dreamed Olivia was with her and awakened reaching out, only to find herself alone in her bed.

Morning was a welcome relief from the torments of the night.

CHAPTER TEN

After a shower, she felt much better. The rest of Sunday passed quickly, with Rebecca determined to stay busy to keep her thoughts of Olivia quieted. She helped her mother clean house, watched the Chiefs football game with her dad, finished her laundry and caught up on all of her studying. She was successful in keeping her mind occupied until that evening when she spent an hour and a half sitting in her bedroom, on the phone with Olivia.

Her mother hadn't probed too deeply about her date, accepting her one-word answers to her questions. *Good, great* and *yeah* had predominated Rebecca's end of the conversation. She had remembered to pass on Olivia's greetings to both of her parents.

* * *

The school week was a short one and it was Thanksgiving Day before Rebecca knew it. She helped her mother prepare their part of the holiday meal and loaded the dishes into the front seat of the Buick. Her parents would ride over to Grandma's in her dad's truck and she would follow, very slowly, of course, to keep from spilling her precious cargo.

Her stomach was rumbling from the aromas of the food by the time she parked in Grandma's back driveway alongside several other cars and trucks. Her mother was waiting for her and they quickly gathered the dishes from the seat and packed the food into the small house, weaving around the smaller children in their path. Some were her younger cousins and some were the children of her older cousins. Inside the house, she nodded to her middle sister, June, who was sitting in Grandma's recliner, holding her six-month-old son, Dean. Her oldest sister, Kate, a nurses' aide at a nursing home in Rockford, was absent—she had to work that day.

When they entered the kitchen, the old table in the center of the small room was bowing from the weight of the abundance of dishes. Rebecca squeezed her dishes in among the others and her mother did the same. Rebecca scanned the selections and saw the normal fare of salads, fried chicken, turkey, stuffing, casseroles, vegetables, dumplings, beans, ham, and, of course, Grandma's famous homemade biscuits. She headed into the utility room off the side of the kitchen and placed her cherry cheesecake on top of the freezer next to the other desserts. She made a mental note of the types of pies and cakes present and vowed to leave room in her stomach for some of each of her favorites. *Man, I love Thanksgiving at Grandma's! I sure wish Olivia could be here for this.*

Grandma stepped into the utility room as she turned away from the desserts. She caught her in her bear hug, then surprised Rebecca by asking, "Why didn't you bring your new friend, Olivia?"

"She had to go to her grandmama's house today, but don't worry, I'll get her down here again to see you. I promise."

"See that you do," she said. "You know, I really enjoyed her visit. It seemed like you two really hit it off, too."

She turned without further explanation of what she meant by *hit it off* and Rebecca followed her back into the madness of the kitchen, pondering her words. Grandma resumed her supervisory role over her daughters, daughters-in-law and granddaughters as they bustled around finishing up the preparations. Rebecca fled as soon as she could duck out the door. She passed through the living room waving quickly to June before she dashed out the front door to the porch. She always felt claustrophobic around that many people, even if they were all family. She knew June would understand why she didn't stay to chat.

"I see you got away without being put to work," Uncle Jim teased her from his perch on the porch railing. She placed her hands behind her on the railing and hoisted herself up to sit beside him.

"Guess I got lucky," she said with a grin. Three of her uncles, one aunt and several cousins were gathered on or around the porch, chatting about a million different topics while watching the young kids play in the yard. It was a little warmer today, with a high of fifty-six degrees forecast. Some years Thanksgiving had been freezing cold, raining, or even snowing, and then they had all packed into the house. That had been nearly too much for Rebecca to handle, so she was grateful for the weather this year.

It wasn't long before they were called inside to fix their plates, then everyone found a place to sit or stand while they ate.

She emptied two heaping plates of food before she headed to the utility room for dessert. After three small pieces of pie, a brownie and a small corner of cherry cheesecake, she called it quits. She fell onto the sofa beside her dad, moaning at the discomfort below her ribs.

He rubbed his stomach and laughed. "Did you overdo it, Bec?"

"I think so," she complained. She was so full, she couldn't move fast enough to escape when she saw two of her aunts burst through the kitchen doorway.

"There's one," she heard as she struggled to get up from the sofa. It was too late. She looked across the room for help but June only laughed at her dilemma, knowing she herself had a pardon due to holding her son. The aunts caught her by both arms and pulled her to her feet, then dragged her into the kitchen, depositing her in front of a sink overflowing with dirty dishes. They left her there to start washing as they headed off after their next victim. Rebecca knew better than to run now. Her aunts were pretty tough.

Soon Rebecca was joined by four other cousins, each arriving in as undignified a manner as she had and each too intimidated by the older generation to resist. They put away food, washed, dried and put away dishes and cleaned the kitchen as best they could. The aunts sat around the table and talked and laughed as they supervised the work of their younger charges. It took over an hour, but they finally gained the approval of the bosses and were allowed to leave.

Normally, Rebecca hated kitchen duty at Grandma's. This year, however, had proven very beneficial. She had overheard Aunt Patsy talking about going shopping on Black Friday in St. Louis. She was meeting her daughter there and they were planning to make a day of it. Rebecca hated to shop, but if she could think of an excuse, maybe she could ride to the city with her and spend the day with Olivia. Her mind was spinning, trying to think of a reason that her aunt would believe without a lot of questions. Her thoughts were interrupted by the chirping of her phone. When she read the text from Olivia, she knew she had her reason.

Grandmama on her way to ER. heart attack? Hope I haven't killed her.

Rebecca rushed outside to a quiet corner of the yard and called Olivia. When she answered, she and her parents were hurrying to the hospital behind the screaming ambulance. Rebecca could tell from the sound of her voice she couldn't go into more details. "Call me later when you know more," Rebecca said. "I'm coming up there tomorrow, I think, if you want me to."

Olivia sounded heartened by this and told her good-bye, promising to call as soon as possible with news. Rebecca turned back toward the house and saw her mother walking across the yard to meet her. "I saw you dash out," she explained. "You look upset, what's wrong?"

Rebecca explained that Olivia's grandmother may have had a heart attack and was on her way to the ER in an ambulance. "Do you think I can ride up with Aunt Patsy tomorrow to make sure Olivia is okay?" she asked. "Aunt Patsy's going up to shop."

"Let's go ask her," her mother said, linking her arm through Rebecca's and leading her back toward the busy house. With her mother's help, she had all the details worked out in a few minutes. As far as Aunt Patsy and the others knew, she would be going to the city to meet a friend from school. Rebecca would ask Olivia if she could pick her up at one of the malls they expected to visit. Being there for Olivia was incentive enough for Rebecca to risk having to shop for a while.

When she headed out through the living room again, June caught up with her. She had put the baby in his carrier in the bedroom for a nap and this was the first opportunity she had to talk to Rebecca. "So, Sis, what's up? Did I hear you are going to St. Louis shopping?" she asked, incredulous.

"Well, yeah, kinda." Rebecca didn't think her sister was going to let her off that easy and she was right.

"Then I don't know my little sister as well as I think I do. I know perfectly well that you hate to shop. What gives?"

Rebecca grabbed her by the elbow and steered her outside, away from all interested ears. "I'm going up to see a friend. I can't go into more details than that here." She scanned the relatives milling around the yard to indicate their lack of privacy.

"Ooh, sounds like I need to stop by the house on my way home this evening," June said, looking at Rebecca, her eyes filled with intrigue. Rebecca blushed slightly but didn't respond. "Okay," June continued, reading her sister's face. "I am definitely coming over to talk to you this evening." Rebecca didn't argue, knowing it would be futile. She headed back into the house to see Grandma before starting home.

About a half-hour later, she made it to her car after saying multiple good-byes and giving more hugs than she thought possible. She told her mother and Grandma she had to study, but when she got home she found studying impossible. She sat at the kitchen table with her books open in front of her and stared out the back door at the pasture beyond. Concern over Olivia and over what she was going to tell June clouded her thoughts and she waited anxiously for the phone to ring or for June to arrive.

June didn't take long to follow her. She left Dean with their mother and Dean's father, although he was still napping and probably would remain asleep for another hour or two.

She heard June pull up in front of the house and waited at the door for her. Her older sister had become a mother for the first time only months before and Rebecca was relieved to see she finally was looking healthy again. The pregnancy hadn't been an easy one. She had looked years older in Rebecca's estimation by the time Dean was born. Three months of interrupted sleep after he was born hadn't helped any. J.T., her husband, had really chipped in, though, taking on his share of the night time duties so she could rest. This was the first time in months that Rebecca had seen her when she didn't appear about ready to drop from fatigue.

She followed June down the hall to the kitchen. Rebecca found it hard to meet her gaze when she sat down at the table across from her.

"Mom said you were out with a friend Saturday night when I called, but she wouldn't go into more details. She said I had to ask you about it. And now you're headed to St. Louis for the day to see a friend. Is this the same friend?"

June had quickly added things together and Rebecca knew why she had never been able to keep secrets from her.

"Yeah," Rebecca answered this question easily. She took a deep breath and plunged ahead. "Her name is Olivia. I met her about a month ago."

"Oh." June sounded a little surprised and looked a little disappointed. "I thought maybe you had finally met someone special." She had often suggested guys from the area Rebecca might be interested in but her ideas had always been rejected by her younger sister.

Rebecca took another deep breath and decided not to lie. "Well, June, I think I have."

"No, Bec, you know what I mean, a boyfriend," she said and laughed. She stopped suddenly when she saw that Rebecca wasn't laughing.

Rebecca leaned forward with her elbows on her knees, clasped her hands in front of her and stared at a spot on the floor a few inches past the ends of her fingers. She searched for the right words to say, to get her point across without upsetting her sister more than necessary. "June, you know I've always been different from you and Kate. I'm figuring out more all the time just how different I am." She paused and took a deep breath, then plunged ahead. "I am really interested in Olivia, you know, like a girlfriend, and she likes me, too."

The kitchen was silent for several seconds and Rebecca looked up to see June staring out the window. Her face displayed the multitude of emotions she was sorting through—confusion, pain, and even understanding vied for control.

Finally, Rebecca could wait no longer. "Say something, June."

"Do Mom and Dad know?"

"I think Mom figured out how I felt before I did. You know how she reads our minds. But I don't know what she has or hasn't told Dad. I haven't said anything, but he's probably noticed a change in my moods."

June had nodded at her comment about their mother. "Well, Bec, I don't really think I understand. Are you sure about this? I mean, do you think this is permanent, or just a one-person thing or what?"

Rebecca understood June's questions because she had asked herself the same questions. "I don't know. I think it's probably just who I am. You know, when I think back over the past several years, it all makes a lot more sense when I think of myself as attracted to women instead of men."

June thought for a minute or two, nodded again. "I guess I can see what you mean. I just didn't think I would ever have a sister who was a...who liked women."

The two sisters finally looked at each other.

"I think the word is lesbian, June," Rebecca said, trying to inject a teasing quality into her tone. "But, do me a favor, would you? Let me tell Dad and Kate on my own time. I want to be sure before I do, and this is all still pretty new to me, too."

"Sure, Bec. Can I tell J.T., though? He'll keep it to himself if I threaten him. I'll just tell him I'll cut him off sex for a month if he talks, and he'll keep his mouth shut." She laughed as Rebecca blushed. "We promised to never keep things from each other, or I wouldn't ask."

"I guess you can." Rebecca was a little unsure about her brother-in-law keeping his silence, but she didn't want to put her sister in a spot in her marriage, either. "I do want you to meet Olivia, though. I think you'll like her. Mom and Dad do. Dad even gave her a grand tour of his machine shed."

"She's not one of those really butch women, is she?" June said, suddenly sounding worried.

"No, not at all." Now it was Rebecca's turn to laugh. "I think I fit that description much better than she ever would. She is actually very pretty." She described her as best she could to June.

"If I didn't believe you before, I do now," June said. "I can tell how much she means to you by the look in your eyes when you talk about her. Be careful, little sister, don't get your heart broken," she cautioned. "After all, you just met her."

"I'm trying to take it slow, June. But it's really hard to do," she admitted.

The phone rang, interrupting their conversation. June answered it, spoke briefly then hung up. "Well, duty calls. Gotta go, Sis. Dean is awake." She gave Rebecca a tight hug, giving her an extra squeeze before letting go. "Love you, Bec. Call if you need to talk."

"Thanks, June." Rebecca felt moisture gathering in the corners of her eyes. "Love you, too."

After June left, Rebecca was able to study a little, but concern for Olivia still interrupted her thoughts frequently.

By the time her parents arrived home, she had given up on studying and was wandering through the house. Her father said nothing but looked up questioningly when she entered the living room a couple of times on her route. Her mother tired quickly of Rebecca's aimless pacing and insisted she play cards with her. She played half-heartedly and checked her phone occasionally to make sure it was working.

It was late that evening before Olivia called. Rebecca answered it before anyone even had a chance to recognize the ring tone. Her mother was relieved to see some of the tension drain from Rebecca's face as she listened to Olivia.

Olivia explained all of the medical details, finally summarizing that it was a mild heart attack and her grandmama would be in the hospital for a few days, but was expected to make a full recovery. The doctors had indicated it was due to a combination of high cholesterol and high blood pressure. Olivia reported her grandmama had been previously diagnosed and had been prescribed medications for both, but thought she knew better than her doctors so had refused to fill the prescriptions. Olivia's mother had assured her that the heart attack had nothing to do with any stress Olivia may have caused, regardless of what her grandmama wanted her to think.

"What happened?" Rebecca asked, trying to understand Olivia's concerns about guilt.

"She caught me pumping Uncle Steve for information," Olivia began, suddenly sounding very tired. "That's what started it all, but it's really a long story. Did you say something about coming here tomorrow or was I hallucinating? I can explain it all then."

"Yeah, I'm going to hitch a ride with Aunt Patsy," Rebecca said excitedly. "Can you pick me up at the St. Louis Outlet Mall?"

"What time?" Olivia answered, sounding like she'd caught her second wind at the prospect of Rebecca's visit.

"Well, the earlier the better," Rebecca said. "I hate shopping. Aunt Patsy wants to be there by five and we're going to Cabela's first. I'll text you where we are."

"I'll pick you up at seven for breakfast," Olivia offered. "That will only be a couple of hours of torture for you. You can survive that long, can't you?"

Rebecca groaned. "I guess I can. But you have to buy breakfast if I have to wait that long."

They laughed and joked for a few more minutes but Rebecca could hear the fatigue creeping back into Olivia's voice. She suggested they get some rest for the early day to follow and wished Olivia a good night and sweet dreams.

She updated her mother on Olivia's grandmother's condition before hugging her goodnight and heading off for bed. She was meeting Aunt Patsy at 2:30 a.m. and that wasn't too many hours away.

CHAPTER ELEVEN

This was it, she was sure she couldn't take another step. Rebecca collapsed onto a bench in the mall as her Aunt Patsy dashed ahead, a bag over each arm, shouting her destination over her shoulder so Rebecca could find her. She had managed to keep up with her shop-a-holic aunt for one hour. *Only one more to go*, she thought, looking at her watch.

Her vision was suddenly blocked as two hands covered her eyes. She nearly leapt to her feet in surprise, but relaxed when she recognized the soft and silky, "Guess who?" whispered in her ear.

She reached up and grabbed the hands, pulling Olivia around the bench, laughing, to sit beside her. Her green eyes sparkled with merriment and Rebecca was struck again by her radiant beauty.

"Surprised you, didn't I?" She smiled mischievously at Rebecca.

"Maybe for a second." Rebecca laughed, shaking off the spell she'd fallen under at the sight of her. "I'm so glad you're early. Now I can get out of this mall."

"Not so fast!" Olivia stopped her, pulling her back down onto the bench. "I'm early so I can shop, too. This is one thing we are *not* going to agree on, Rebecca Wilcox. You obviously hate to shop. I, however, do not. So, where is Aunt Patsy?"

She stood and looked around at the crowd expectantly, waiting for Rebecca to guide her. Rebecca could tell from the determined look on her face that she had lost this argument before it even got started. Besides, she wasn't sure she wanted to deny Olivia something that meant so much to her. She stood and took Olivia's hand, leading her along the path she had watched her Aunt Patsy take only minutes before.

Aunt Patsy was thrilled to meet Olivia and the two shoppers spent the next hour digging through piles of clothes, exclaiming over bargains and congratulating each other on their good taste and good fortune. As she laughed at the antics of the self-confessed addicts, Rebecca even found herself having fun. About a half hour after Olivia had arrived, her cousin caught up with them and Rebecca decided the apple hadn't fallen far from the tree when it came to her two relatives and their shopping.

At a few minutes after seven, Olivia caught Rebecca looking at her watch. "Oh," Olivia exclaimed. "Ladies, I'm afraid you'll have to continue without us. I promised Rebecca breakfast at seven and I'm already late."

Her shopping cohorts expressed their disappointment but said they understood, and Rebecca began to breathe a little easier. After quick hugs, with Aunt Patsy promising to call Rebecca so they could meet at the end of the day, they headed for the registers. Rebecca shifted anxiously from foot-to-foot as she stood behind Olivia in the long lines at the registers. When they finally finished checking out, she couldn't help but increase the pace of her steps as she neared the exits.

Olivia grabbed her elbow as she struggled to keep up with Rebecca's longer strides. "You really don't like to shop, do you? I thought you were exaggerating."

"I just prefer more open places," Rebecca explained, slowing down as they entered the crisp November air outside the mall. "But if you want to shop, I'll grin and bear it," she added, smiling sheepishly.

"No, I think I've fed my shopping bug enough for today," Olivia said. "Let's eat."

"Now you're talking my language," Rebecca said with a laugh. "Take me to some pancakes."

Rebecca kept Olivia laughing throughout their breakfast at the local pancake house. She recounted some of the livelier events of the previous day at her Grandma's gathering. Olivia seemed to like the part about her capture by her aunts for kitchen duty. She remembered to tell her about Grandma's words about her, also, and that she really wanted her to visit again.

Afterward, they headed south for ten minutes on the interstate then they exited into a suburban residential area. Olivia turned onto a quiet street and pulled up in front of a three-story brick house which had been converted into apartments. She led Rebecca up to the second floor and unlocked the door, motioning for Rebecca to step in ahead of her.

Rebecca noticed a comfortable living room with a small table near the back right corner and a small kitchen inset opposite it. Two doors on her right she surmised were a bedroom and a bathroom. In an easy chair, she spied a large gray cat curled up with his tail resting in front of his eyes, undisturbed by their arrival.

"This must be Pooh," she exclaimed, scooping the startled feline into her arms, settling onto the easy chair with Pooh nestled in her lap. She stroked the cat and quickly identified the places behind his ears and under his chin that he couldn't resist having scratched. Olivia watched Rebecca's deft fingers with a smile, then turned and opened her bedroom door to place her packages inside. She removed her coat and waited as Rebecca stopped her petting duties long enough to remove her jacket.

Olivia puttered around in the kitchen making coffee then brought in two steaming cups and placed them on coasters on the end table between the sofa and the easy chair. She sighed deeply as she sank down onto the end of the sofa, kicked her shoes off and curled her legs up under her.

Olivia sipped her coffee in silence and Rebecca didn't push her. She continued to pet the cat.

"Yesterday was a nightmare," Olivia finally began. "It started out okay. You knew my parents were coming to visit and Uncle Steve and his family live here in the city, so they were at Grandmama's also." She paused to sip coffee.

"Mom and Grandmama were busy in the dining room setting the table, so I cornered Uncle Steve in the living room. I mentioned I had a friend in Springtown and that got his attention. Before he knew it, he admitted he had been there before."

"Wow," Rebecca said. "I wonder what he was doing there? It's not exactly a tourist attraction."

"That's what I was wondering, too. I pushed a little harder and asked if he knew any of the Farthings from Springtown. For a second I thought he'd swallowed his tongue. He turned beet red then really white, like he was going to pass out. He denied it, but I know he knows more than he'd say."

"What set your grandmama off?" Rebecca asked, guessing it was something Olivia had said.

"Well, I think she overheard me say the name Farthing. I thought I heard a gasp and when I turned around, she was standing in the doorway. But she didn't say anything, just walked back toward the dining room. Then, during our dinner, Mom asked how my trip out of town had been, you know, the weekend I stayed with you. I'd told her I met you in Rockford, so I guess that's where she thought you lived. I was telling them about your family's farming operation and about how large your extended family is. Then Grandmama asked where you lived. I guess she put it together with what she'd overheard earlier. Well, I guess I took a page from Uncle Steve's book, because I answered before I even thought about it."

She took another sip of coffee then continued. "Grandmama gave Mom and Uncle Steve a funny look when I said Springtown then she asked how I knew you. I guess she read more into it than I meant to give away. I said you were my good friend, that we met at a meeting and hit it off. Maybe something showed in my face or my Mom's face, I don't know. But Grandmama went off the deep end. She said she wouldn't stand for one of her granddaughters to carry on with some female country bumpkin from a little hick town where people didn't know right from wrong.

"I'm sorry," Olivia said as she saw the brief flicker of pain cross Rebecca's face at the insult to her and her home town.

"It'll be okay," Rebecca reassured her. "Keep on with your story."

"Well, that's about the end of it. Grandmama grabbed her chest and kind of stared off into space then she slid down in her chair. Uncle Steve was sitting next to her and he caught her before she fell into the floor. I don't think she passed out completely, but she couldn't sit up by herself. Dad ran to the phone and called 911, and Mom and Uncle Steve tended to Grandmama until the paramedics came and took over. I thought maybe my parents would talk to me about what happened while we were driving to the hospital but they didn't say anything, except after you called. Mom asked who'd called and I said it was you. All she said was, 'Okay.'"

Rebecca had been sipping her coffee when Olivia finished her story and she looked up in time to see a tear trickle down Olivia's cheek. She set Pooh in the chair and rose to sit beside Olivia on the sofa. Olivia put her head under Rebecca's chin and cried softly into the front of her soft flannel shirt. Rebecca held her and gently stroked her hair and her back, gently making shushing sounds to soothe her as Olivia released some of the pain she had been holding inside. Eventually the tears subsided but still they sat together, Olivia seeming to draw strength from the comfort of Rebecca's arms around her. "You know you can't be responsible for how other people react, don't you?" Rebecca asked her quietly.

"I know, but I still feel guilty." Olivia sniffled a little. "I love my Grandmama and I feel like I just lost her, somehow."

"Are you going to the hospital today?" Rebecca asked softly.

"No. Mom said she was going this morning and would be coming here this afternoon to let me know how Grandmama is doing. She and Dad stayed at Grandmama's house last night. She suggested it might be best to wait a couple of days before I try going to see her so maybe she'll cool down a little bit."

"Is it okay that I'm here today?" Rebecca asked, suddenly worried she may have added to Olivia's troubles. "Will your mom be upset?"

"I don't know if it's okay with her," Olivia said, her voice suddenly filled with determination. "But it's okay with me. Before yesterday, I would have said it wouldn't upset her but now I don't know. I think the time has come, though, for me to stand my ground. You being here is part of who I am, part of my life. They're going to have to learn to accept that." Olivia's eyes had an unyielding look and while Rebecca was worried about a possible confrontation, she was also proud of Olivia's decision to stand strong.

Family was very important to Rebecca and she hoped she never had to decide between her family and her freedom to live her own life. If so, she might need lessons from Olivia with her inner steel. "You know I'll do whatever you want," Rebecca offered. "I can disappear while she's here or I'll stand beside you for moral support, it's your call."

"Right now, what I want you to do is…" Olivia said, as the expression on her face changed to one of excitement. She pulled out of Rebecca's embrace and stood. "Grab your coat and come shopping with me again."

"Shopping, again?" Rebecca tried not to whine. "But I thought you said—"

"Grocery shopping, you goofball! I know you love food, so surely you can stand some grocery shopping." Olivia laughed and pulled her to the door.

CHAPTER TWELVE

Rebecca had never been to an organic market, but as they searched the aisles for something that screamed lunch, she decided if she had to live in a city, she would frequent this kind of place. It was like shopping at a giant farmers market, only cleaner and all indoors.

They agreed on several ingredients for a chef's salad and when they returned to Olivia's apartment, they shared the work of putting together their meal. Rebecca filled two glasses with cherry Coke, their one indiscretion with the healthy meal.

They carried the fruits of their labor to the table and sat close together to eat. Rebecca rubbed her knee against Olivia's, hoping the contact was causing the same riot of sensations in Olivia as it was in her. Olivia didn't say anything, just looked up from her salad and smiled that funny smile. "Let's listen to some music," Olivia suggested after lunch. She showed Rebecca her collection of CDs in a tower beside her stereo. "I've got stuff downloaded onto my computer, if you don't see something you like there."

Rebecca chose several CDs. Olivia placed them into the stereo then randomized their play order. When the music started, Olivia said, "Do you dance? I mean, it's okay if you don't, because I'd love to teach you." She smiled suggestively.

Rebecca had been to school dances before but had done more talking than dancing. "I'm not sure you could call it dancing," she admitted, fighting the blush overtaking her cheeks at Olivia's light flirting.

"Okay," Olivia laughed. "Well, let's find out." She pulled Rebecca to the middle of the room and started moving to the music. Rebecca attempted to imitate her moves but could tell from the laughter in Olivia's eyes that her dancing left something to be desired.

"That's it," she said, laughing as the song ended. "I think you've had enough fun at my expense."

Olivia grabbed her hand. "Wait, one more. This is a slow one. Let me lead, just hold on and follow me."

As foolish as she felt during the faster dance, this slow dance with Olivia felt much more like something she could learn to appreciate. She felt awkward and stiff at first, but soon the feel of Olivia's soft body under her hands, her breath against her neck, her head resting on Rebecca's shoulder as they moved back and forth around the small room, had Rebecca worrying less about her dancing skills and more about how to get closer. She followed Olivia's lead and found herself able to move with her to the beat. She was disappointed when the song ended and another fast song began. Rebecca didn't release Olivia's hand as she stepped over to the sofa and Olivia didn't protest, sitting down sideways across her lap. Rebecca had just touched her lips to Olivia's when the doorbell rang. Rebecca jumped at the sound. Olivia just groaned in disappointment.

"Oh, no. That's probably Mom," Olivia said, rising slowly to her feet. She turned the music down, looked around the room to be sure everything was in order and gave Rebecca a reassuring nod and wink before she went to open the door.

Rebecca heard her greet her mother and Olivia introduced them as her mother entered the room. "It's nice to meet you,

Mrs. Harmon," Rebecca said politely, standing and reaching out to shake her hand.

"You can call me Eliza if you like," she said warmly. "I understand you and Olivia are becoming quite close," she continued, gently moving the cat from his perch and settling into the easy chair. She placed her coat beside her chair, but Olivia retrieved it and hung it on the coat rack before returning to her seat on the sofa, sitting stiffly beside Rebecca.

Eliza addressed Rebecca briefly before turning her attention to her daughter. "I'm glad Olivia has someone to lean on right now." She continued without pause, "Olivia, I hope you believe you're not responsible for Grandmama's heart attack. She has to accept full responsibility for it. This morning the doctor said her heart was a ticking time bomb, but if she'd taken the medicine she'd been prescribed, this heart attack would have probably never happened. Also, I want you to know that I don't agree with Grandmama. She said some very hurtful things to you yesterday and she had no right."

Rebecca saw tears escaping, slowly trickling down Olivia's face. She reached out and squeezed her hand, pulling it over onto her thigh so she could keep it between her own hands.

Eliza noticed the caring gesture and smiled slightly before she continued, this time more slowly and in a gentler tone. "It's hard to explain, but Grandmama thinks she's justified in the way she feels. You know Gran raised her as a single parent. And she never knew her father. But there's a part of her story she doesn't want anyone to know. I think it's about time you learned her whole story."

Olivia wiped her tears with a tissue and gave her mother her full attention. Rebecca was equally caught up by the tone of Eliza's voice, anticipating a deep secret about to be revealed.

"I know you overheard me talking to your uncle on the phone that day and I assume that's what got your curiosity aroused. Uncle Steve told me you were asking questions about Springtown and the Farthings. He never could keep a secret," she complained. "Anyway, Mary Farthing from Springtown and your Gran were friends all those years ago. When Gran was growing older, she told me all about it. Mary, or MJ, as Gran called her, had moved to St. Louis to attend a business school then stayed here in the city to work. She met Gran while she was in school. They fell in love, you see."

Eliza only paused momentarily as Olivia and Rebecca both gasped. "At that time it was dangerous for two women to be exposed as lovers. But they'd taken the risk and lived in the same house together for five years in the late nineteen twenties and early thirties, until Mary died. They tried to keep it a secret, but rumors got out and even after Mary died people still talked."

Both Rebecca and Olivia sat stunned at the news, an undreamed of possibility when they had speculated about what might have been.

"What happened to her, Mom?" Olivia whispered. "How did she die?"

"During childbirth," her mother explained.

It took a few moments for Olivia to grasp the import of her explanation. Then she gasped and exclaimed, "Oh, my gosh! You mean…? I knew I recognized the date on that headstone."

Rebecca still had a puzzled expression on her face, and now Eliza did too.

"What do you mean, on the headstone? You've seen Mary Farthing's headstone?" she questioned.

"Yes, Mom! Rebecca took me to Peacock Cemetery and we figured out from that old picture of Gran's who MJ was from the house in the background."

Rebecca was still feeling like she had missed something important. "Can we back up a minute?" she interrupted. "What's this about the date on the headstone?"

Olivia was practically bouncing as she waited for her mother to explain. "Mary Farthing died giving birth to Grandmama. Olivia recognized her birth date as Mary's date of death. But why were you in Peacock Cemetery?"

"Wow!" Rebecca let the word slip out. Now she hastened to recover and explain about the cemetery. "I took her to see it when she came to visit. It's in a field right by my uncle's house and it's supposed to be haunted. But if Mary was Grandmama's mother, then was Ralph her father?"

Eliza looked puzzled. "Ralph who?"

"Remember, Mom? I told you we had an old picture with Gran and Mary in it. Well, there was this guy standing beside Mary and the back of the picture identified him as Ralph. We found out the Farthings had a farm hand named Ralph Dunlop."

"Honestly girls, I don't know. I asked Gran once who my grandfather was and she didn't answer. I know she heard me, but she turned her back to me and walked out of the room. I thought I heard her crying, but I couldn't be sure. She never told me and I was too afraid of upsetting her to ask. I doubt it was a planned pregnancy. The stigma of being an unwed mother would have only added to that associated with two unwed young women spending their lives together."

Rebecca thought any of the other ways she could think of for a woman to become pregnant in nineteen thirty-two would be sufficient to cause her lover to weep. *Had Mary been seeing a man behind Gran's back? Had Mary been raped?*

"Do you think Grandmama knows who her father is and what the story is behind her conception?" Olivia asked.

"I don't know. And I know better than to ask," Eliza said firmly. "Your Grandmama won't talk about Gran and Mary at all. Let me finish and maybe you'll understand why." Eliza continued the story in a more somber tone. "Gran was heartbroken but raised Mary's baby as her own. Her family had enough influence that no one openly questioned the situation, but the scandalous whispers persisted throughout the years Grandmama was growing up. They never bothered Gran. She'd built a wall around her heart when Mary died and it was only in her final few years that she started letting her closest family inside that wall. Grandmama had much thinner skin. She had fewer defenses as a child and a young woman and was often hurt by the rumors."

"Poor Grandmama." Olivia was nearing tears again. "And Gran was probably too wrapped up in her own grief to notice how it affected Grandmama."

"Exactly," her mother confirmed. "Grandmama felt like if Gran and Mary had never been lovers, her life would have been easier, less painful. And I'm sure she's right. But it all started when Gran met a girl from Springtown. That's why she was so upset when she heard you talking about your friend from Springtown."

Olivia thought for a few seconds then responded. "I guess I understand, Mom, but I don't know how I can keep from disappointing or upsetting her. I can't change who I am...or how I feel about Rebecca." She smiled at Rebecca and squeezed her hand.

"Well, let's try to give her a little time," her mother suggested. "Maybe she'll change her mind," she said hopefully.

Olivia's eyes were clouded with doubt, but she tried to sound upbeat as she agreed to wait and see.

* * *

Olivia's mother left shortly afterward to return to the hospital but promised to return the following day to talk to Olivia further about Gran and Grandmama. Rebecca had stifled her desire to ask more questions but her mind was racing with them. She asked Olivia to get her notebook from the bedroom and she moved over to the table. Olivia returned with the notebook and sat down next to her.

"May I make a few entries?" she asked Olivia.

Olivia turned to the first blank pages and handed her a pen. "Of course," she said, watching closely to see what Rebecca might write.

"I want to make a list of all the questions we initially had," she explained. "Then we'll know exactly where we stand. We can see what questions are left unanswered."

"Okay, that sounds like a good idea," Olivia agreed. She was relieved to have something constructive take her attention away from the rift between her and her grandmother.

Rebecca wrote quietly for a few minutes then handed the list she had compiled to Olivia.

1)Who was MJ and how was she connected to Jane Smith?
Mary J. Farthing, lover of Jane Smith, mother of infant

daughter raised by Jane Smith as her own after death of Mary during childbirth.

2)Who was Ralph and how was he connected?

Ralph Dunlop, hired hand of Farthing family, left town after dispute with Mr. Farthing.

3)What was the secret Eliza and Steve were talking about on the phone?

4)Did something happen recently at Mary's grave?

"Are there any questions you can think of that we need to investigate?" Rebecca asked.

"I have a couple I want to add," Olivia said, as she grabbed the pen and bent over the notebook. She quickly jotted down her ideas then showed them to Rebecca.

5)Who was the father of Mary's baby, and how does he fit into the picture? Why didn't he step forward to help out?

6)Who did we hear laughing? Is Peacock Cemetery really haunted?

"Yeah," Rebecca said. "Do you think we'll ever figure out the last one?"

"I don't know, but stranger things have happened," Olivia said optimistically. "Maybe we can call one of those paranormal investigator groups and have them check it out," she jested lightly.

Rebecca chuckled then became more somber. "I'm sorry, you know," she said softly, putting her hands over Olivia's. "About your grandmama being so upset with you, I mean. You know I would never want to cause problems or pain for you."

"Oh, Rebecca," Olivia cried out. "You aren't causing the rift. I am who I am regardless of your presence or absence. Grandmama is causing the rift with her attitude toward Gran coloring the way she views the world, even allowing it to ruin her relationship with me."

Rebecca gently pulled on Olivia's arms, guiding her over to sit on her lap again while she held her and tried to soothe her. "Maybe your mom will be able to get through to her," she said. "Don't give up on her."

Olivia rested her forehead against the side of Rebecca's head. "I hope you're right," she said.

They tried to renew their interest in the music, but both were too distracted by their own thoughts after the revelations of the afternoon. Eventually, they ended up on the sofa, Rebecca sitting at one end with Olivia's head resting in her lap. Rebecca absently played with Olivia's hair, curling locks of it around her fingers. She carefully traced the lines of her face, trying to memorize every detail to carry home with her. Olivia stared at a spot on the wall in front of them, her mind apparently centered on the events of decades past.

They were both startled when Rebecca's ring tone sounded. Aunt Patsy was finally shopped out. She offered to stop by Olivia's apartment and pick up Rebecca, so Olivia took the phone and gave her the address to enter into her GPS. Olivia closed the phone and returned it to Rebecca.

"I'm sorry if today's been sort of a bummer for you," she said, placing an arm around Rebecca as she moved to sit close to her. "I'll have to try and make it up to you somehow."

This time when their lips touched, Rebecca felt more than desire in Olivia. Olivia's pain at the denial by her grandmother was evident in her kiss. Rebecca responded carefully, holding Olivia tightly and allowing her to take from her as a bee takes nectar from a flower.

Rebecca felt Olivia's need easing in the kiss and relaxed her embrace. She leaned back slightly to look into Olivia's eyes. Tears welled in their corners, but some of the sparkle she loved was starting to return. "Will you be okay?" Rebecca asked. "If you're not, I'm not going to leave. I'll call Mom and Dad and see if they can come and get me in a day or two."

"I would love for you to stay," Olivia said, holding Rebecca's face between her hands. "But I'm going to be okay. I know it's a lot to ask to have your parents come after you. And we both need to study. I doubt if we would do that even if you had your books here. At least I'd have a problem concentrating on boring textbooks with you sitting across the table from me." She smiled and gave Rebecca a quick peck then dropped her hands down to hold Rebecca's.

"I want you to go home with Aunt Patsy like you planned. Maybe I can get some of this worked out this weekend with

Mom's help. Thank you though, for offering. You are a sweetheart, you know."

"I can see how much this has upset you and I'd do anything to take that pain away," Rebecca vowed.

"I believe that," Olivia asserted. She leaned forward and kissed her again. No pain was evident in this kiss, only hopefulness and promise.

Rebecca reluctantly released her hands and stood to gather her things. Aunt Patsy should be there any moment. She saw her pull up to the curb in front of the building, turned to kiss Olivia quickly good-bye, then left as Olivia had asked before she could change her mind and argue to stay.

If Aunt Patsy noticed her niece's subdued manner, she didn't comment. She rattled on about her shopping exploits and Rebecca was glad she had little need to contribute to the conversation. By the time she reached home, she had never felt more drained.

When she stumbled into the house, her parents had just finished supper. Rebecca was too tired to eat and declined her mother's offer of a sandwich.

She promised to catch her up on the day's events the next morning, texted Olivia she had made it home safely, then went to her room. She stretched out on her bed fully clothed and was asleep the second her head hit the pillow.

CHAPTER THIRTEEN

Rebecca awoke feeling groggy and slightly disoriented. For a moment she couldn't remember where she was and why she was still wearing her shirt and jeans. She stared at the ceiling and the fog slowly cleared from her thoughts. The events of the previous day replayed through her mind. Olivia sure had a lot of things to sort through. She didn't envy her the confrontation she realized must come. She knew Olivia was determined to live her own life and wasn't willing to hide her feelings from Grandmama any longer. Yet, based on what Eliza had disclosed, if Grandmama were to accept Olivia for who she was, she would have to overcome a lifetime of pain, pain from growing up with a distant mother and pain from the scandalous whispers of others.

Rebecca also wondered where her own feelings for Olivia would lead. Previously, they had flirted and found an obvious sexual attraction toward one another, but yesterday had been different. They had bonded on a different level, sharing a spectrum of emotions from pain to hope. Rebecca felt a growing love for Olivia and thought Olivia felt the same way toward her. Rebecca felt afraid to express it—she didn't know what she would do if it wasn't reciprocal. She tried imagining several scenarios for how the next few years would go and felt reassured that placing Olivia into any of them only made the future look brighter.

She realized that now was probably not the time to push Olivia about their relationship. She would have to be patient and allow Olivia to concentrate on her relationship with her grandmama first. Besides, this was Rebecca's first love and her brain kept reminding her heart it was wise for both of them to go slow anyway. She hoped her heart was listening.

Rebecca heard her mother vacuuming in the hallway outside her bedroom door and grinned as she swung her legs over the edge of the bed. Her mother was a creature of habit and Rebecca knew this was not the time of day for her to vacuum.

"Wake up call?" she queried, as she trotted past her mother to the bathroom.

"Oh, I'm sorry. Did I wake you?" her mother asked just a little too innocently.

Rebecca knew her mother was expecting a full rundown of the previous day's events, so she hurriedly showered and changed into fresh clothes. When she entered the kitchen, her mother was sitting at the table behind her newspaper. She couldn't resist the barb, "Finish your vacuuming already?"

After filling her coffee cup, Rebecca sat down at the table and settled in for what she knew would be a long interrogation. Beth folded her newspaper and set it aside, giving Rebecca her undivided attention. Rebecca told her mother all she had learned the previous day. She knew her mother would treat the story as confidential. Beth was not a cog in the local rumor mill. There weren't many around who would remember the Farthing family anyway, so the story certainly wouldn't be much grist for the mill.

As she related the tragic tale, her mother expressed surprise and dismay. Rebecca watched her closely as she repeated the statement made about Olivia carrying on with a country bumpkin from a hick town and noticed the quick flash of anger.

After she finished, she sat back in her chair and sipped her coffee, waiting for her mother's response.

Rebecca's mother reacted with understanding. "It must have been very difficult for Olivia's grandmother when she was growing up. In that day and age, anyone who didn't come from a traditional home could be treated very badly. And to make it worse her mother was unable to comfort and support her. She may not have even noticed her pain. That's a lot for a child to handle. I'm not surprised she reacted the way she did to Olivia's connection to a girl from Springtown."

"I agree, Mom. It's quite a mess. Olivia isn't sure she'll ever come around to accepting it. I don't know what to do for her, how to help."

Beth took Rebecca's hand. "I may not know all the answers but Olivia is going to need time to heal. She's going to need your support, especially if her grandmother persists in her rejection of her. Just be there for her, listen when she needs to talk and don't push her to make choices she may not be ready to make. And if *you* need someone to talk to, remember, I'm always here for you. June told me you told her about you and Olivia. You know she's there for you, too."

Her mother looked directly at Rebecca as she spoke. "I know I haven't come right out and said anything, Bec, because I didn't want to push you to talk until you were ready. I can see you have some very strong feelings for Olivia."

Rebecca nodded but didn't speak.

"I don't know how to ask this, Rebecca. Are you sure what you're feeling is right for you? I mean, are you sure you're… attracted…to women?"

Her mother's voice had been gentle and hesitant. Rebecca knew in her heart she wasn't really questioning her choices, only seeking confirmation, but it still stung a little that she asked.

She nodded and tried to look away, but her mother tugged gently on her hands. "You don't need to look away. I'm not ashamed of you. I'll always love you, for who you are, all of you."

"Thanks, Mom. Not just for this morning. For letting me make my own choices. You know I love you, too." Rebecca squeezed her mother's hands in her own. She could see the love in her mother's eyes and she remembered how Olivia described *her* mother's reaction. Rebecca realized how lucky she was.

She studied her mother now, truly seeing this woman she had called Mom all her life, realizing how much she had taken for granted all these years. She was surprised at the signs of aging she hadn't noticed. The graying at her temples was new—she was sure it hadn't been there a year ago. The creases at the corners of her eyes and mouth were deepening and the reading glasses that used to hang neglected around her neck most of the time were finding their proper place perched on her nose more often now than not. Rebecca hoped her mother hadn't hastened her aging by worrying about her but suspected she had.

Beth interrupted her musings, continuing in the same gentle tone. "I can't say I understand the path you've chosen. It isn't a turn I would've ever taken. After thirty years, I'm as head-over-heels in love with your father as I was the day I married him, possibly even more. I never experienced any of the feelings…" She paused and chose her words carefully. "I never experienced any of the feelings for the same sex that you seem to feel. But I do understand some things about my daughter. You are honest and sincere, compassionate and loving. You would not be trying this lifestyle unless you believed it was right for you. I don't believe you're capable of that much self-deception—"

"I don't know, Mom," Rebecca interrupted. "I think I've done a pretty good job at self-deception the past several years. Trying to be straight."

"Bec, I've watched you struggle with something during all those years. I don't think you were deceiving yourself as well as you thought or you wouldn't have been struggling like that. This past month has been different—you've stopped fighting with yourself. You seem happier with being you. All I ask is that you follow your heart and remember to listen closely to what it tells you, not just about other people but about yourself, as well."

"How did you get so smart?" Rebecca asked, teasing lightly as she stood. She leaned over to hug her mother. "You know, I am truly blessed to have you for a mother."

"I am equally blessed to have you as a daughter," her mother responded. "Now, enough of all this mushy stuff," she said briskly, blinking suddenly to fight her tears. "Sit back down and tell me how you enjoyed shopping with Aunt Patsy."

* * *

Olivia called that evening. She had met again with her mother but she reported no new revelations.

"I had a long talk with my mom today," Rebecca related. "She feels as bad about it all as I do. You know if you need me for anything, I'm there. Or if you need to get away, you're always welcome here."

"Thanks. My mom is being really supportive, too. I think she feels guilty because Grandmama is reacting so harshly. I tried to tell her it's not her fault but I think she still feels bad."

"How is Grandmama?" Rebecca asked.

"Better. Mom thinks she'll come home tomorrow. Mom plans to stay with her for a couple of weeks, maybe through Christmas. Dad's flying home today.

"You know, I think we can find better things to talk about," Olivia said, changing not only the subject but her tone. "So, how was the trip home with Aunt Patsy? I bet she talked your ears off and all about your favorite subject...shopping!" Olivia laughed.

"You're as bad as my mother, tormenting me about Aunt Patsy." Rebecca responded gladly to the change in tone, laughing and joking with Olivia for the next thirty minutes.

CHAPTER FOURTEEN

On Sunday, the world seemed to return to normal for Rebecca. She studied and helped her mother around the house. Her call from Olivia that evening was mostly upbeat. The only time Olivia's voice showed any strain was when she related that Grandmama had returned home, but she still hadn't seen her. Olivia's mother had cautioned her to keep her distance. Grandmama had not calmed down any yet.

The following week went quickly and Rebecca was eager for the end of the semester. Olivia had seemed to brighten each evening during their phone conversations. But their remaining questions about the mysteries were no closer to being answered. Olivia's mother had been there when she called Thursday evening and Eliza had asked to speak to Beth. When Rebecca and Olivia got their phones back, neither knew what had been discussed between the other two women. They weren't sure they liked the idea of their mothers keeping secrets from them, but they were glad they had established some communication between them.

One more week of classes, then finals week, then freedom! Rebecca told herself as she headed home Friday after classes and work. That evening's phone call was even lighter. Olivia teased her over the phone, reminding her of the tree she had pushed her against while she kissed her in the back pasture. By the time they ended their call, Rebecca was nearly as weak-kneed as she had been the day of their picnic. She slept restlessly that night, with Olivia filling her dreams.

* * *

Saturday morning, Rebecca was surprised when she entered the kitchen and didn't find her mother at the table. Her paper remained folded on the side of the table where Rebecca's father always placed it when he brought it to her each morning. When Rebecca turned from filling her coffee cup, her mother was entering the room with her purse and coat.

"Where are you headed so early on a Saturday morning?" Rebecca asked suspiciously.

"Groceries," her mother said simply. "I'll be back in an hour. You're not going anywhere today, are you?"

"I planned on studying most of the day," she admitted. "But if you need me to run an errand for you, I can. I'm really caught up on studying. I'm just trying to be sure I'm ready for finals."

"Good. No, I don't have errands for you. I'm just trying to keep track of you. 'Bye." She grabbed the cup of coffee in the travel mug sitting beside the coffee pot and headed out of the room.

Rebecca looked at the receding figure of her mother in puzzlement. "Now what is she up to?" she said quietly. She walked to the front door to watch her leave. A sound from her dad's recliner in the living room startled her and she nearly spilled her cup of coffee. She turned to see him sitting quietly, reading a farm journal.

"Good morning, Dad," she greeted him. He was nearly always gone by this time of morning, preferring to get out early to check his livestock and machinery. Now she knew something was up. She sat down at the sofa, hoping to pump him for information.

"What's up, Dad? Are we throwing a party or something? Someone forgot to let me in on it."

"You'll have to ask your mother," he said noncommittally, not looking up from his journal.

"Okay." She pretended to look at a magazine on the coffee table. "Are June and Kate coming over?"

"I don't think so."

Rebecca's parents didn't have company often so she wasn't quite sure how to proceed with her questioning. Also, she knew her father could keep a secret better than most.

"How's Olivia doing?" Her father's question jolted her out of her pondering.

"Fine, I guess. Good. I talked to her last night and everything seemed okay." Rebecca wasn't sure what he knew about her and Olivia and wasn't sure how much information she wanted to divulge. On the other hand, she knew she would have to talk to him sometime, so maybe today would be a good time.

"Uh, Dad," she began hesitantly, unsure how she wanted to proceed.

At her tone he looked up questioningly from his journal.

"Dad, there's something I need to talk to you about."

He waited patiently for her to gather her thoughts.

"Um, I guess I should explain a few things about Olivia. And about me, I guess." Rebecca was staring hard at the coffee table. Her mother was much more open with her feelings than her dad had ever been and she wasn't sure how he was going to react to her news. "I guess I've always known I was a little different than June and Kate, but lately, I guess I've found out how different. Dad, I hope you're not disappointed in me, but I think I like women."

There, that was it. I said it.

She took a deep breath and waited for the worst.

Her dad was silent for a few minutes. She could feel him studying her but she still couldn't turn to look at him. When he finally did speak, she jumped as if he had yelled, although his voice was calm and quiet.

"Rebecca, your mother and I have discussed this at length. I'll admit I was surprised at first, but I guess it's starting to sink in. You asked if I'm disappointed. The answer is yes, in some ways."

Rebecca dropped her head down a little and he quickly added, "But not like you think. You see, when you were born I dreamed big dreams for you. I had my ideas of how your life would go. And, honestly, you dating a woman wasn't something I ever dreamed of for you. But as a parent, you learn that your dreams aren't as important to your children as helping them achieve their own dreams. So, yes, I am disappointed that my dreams are not your dreams. But, I'm not disappointed in *you*." He watched to see if she would understand the distinction.

Rebecca nodded slightly, blinking back the tears, determined not to let them fall. "I guess I understand."

"Rebecca, you are my little girl and no matter how old you are you will always be my little girl. My greatest wish for you is to be happy. I hope you can be happy with the choice you've made. I'm concerned that you've chosen a tough row to hoe. People, especially around here, aren't really supportive of that kind of lifestyle, so you're going to have some battles ahead of you. You're old enough now that your mother and I are limited in the battles we can take on for you."

He paused again, swallowed deeply, then asked, "Bec, are you sure this is what's going to make you happy? If you can look at me and tell me it is, I'll support you all I can."

Rebecca pulled back her shoulders, thought of Olivia and her inner steel and turned to meet her father's gaze. "Dad, I'm happier with Olivia than I have been in years. It feels right for me to love her. I really believe this is who I am. A lesbian."

He flinched a little at her last words but she could see he was trying to understand her. "You know, Bec, I'm proud of you. You've always been our strong-willed daughter and you're showing me now that you aren't afraid of doing what's right for you just because it may not be easy. I hope I can be as brave as you about this, but if I falter at times, please forgive me. I love you, girl, just remember that."

"Dad, I love you, too," she said, and this time she couldn't stop the tears.

He placed his journal on the end table beside his chair and held his arms out toward her. She walked over and sat down on his lap. For the first time in many years, she cried on his shoulder while he held her and rocked her gently.

"Your mother is going to skin me," he finally said.

"Why's that?" she sniffled.

"She told me not to get my shirt messed up while she was gone. I do believe you have soaked it thoroughly. At least you don't wear makeup like your sisters. Then it would really be a mess."

"Dad?"

"Yes."

"Thank you for letting me mess up your shirt."

"You're welcome."

"And, Dad?"

"Yes."

"Will you tell me what's going on today?"

"No. I've been sworn to secrecy by your mother. Now, go pick me out another nice shirt from my closet so I can change before she gets back."

She did as he asked and he settled back to reading his journal.

She went to the kitchen, fixed a bowl of cereal and toast and sat at the table, eating quietly, thinking about how lucky she was to be born into her family.

Her mother returned when she was getting ready to feed the cows. Rebecca went outside to help her carry in groceries.

"What's up, Mom?" she asked, putting frozen vegetables in the freezer.

"Company is coming for lunch," she said, "but that is all you're going to get out of me. I suggest you hustle and get all your outside chores done, then head to the shower and get cleaned up before they get here."

Rebecca was really puzzled over their mystery guests but she did as her mother asked. After feeding the cattle, she hurried through the shower. She had heard her parents talking in the other room when she returned from outside and assumed her dad was telling her mom about their conversation. Her assumption was proven correct when her mother came in and gave her a hug after her shower, while she was getting dressed. "I'm glad you talked to your father," was all she said.

Rebecca had just slipped into a pair of black jeans and a long-sleeved blue sweater when she heard a car pull up in front of the house. Her bedroom windows faced the rear of the house so she couldn't peek out to identify the newcomers. She grabbed a comb from the dresser and quickly flipped her hair into a semblance of order.

She heard voices at the front door and stepped into the hallway just in time to see Olivia making her way toward her. Olivia smiled that funny smile and winked at Rebecca. "Hi, Bec. Surprise!"

Olivia laughed at the look of confusion on Rebecca's face, followed by surprise then pleasure as she drank in the sight of Olivia. She looked great in a red V-neck dress that wasn't so short to be daring but showed enough cleavage and thigh to cause Rebecca's pulse to quicken. She blinked as she saw her mother right behind Olivia and realized she could see the look of desire she knew must show on her face. She reined in her thoughts quickly and hoped she had regained control of her expressions, because Eliza stepped into the hallway directly behind Beth. She wanted to rush up and embrace Olivia, but was too embarrassed to do so in front of their mothers. Olivia, however, was more sure of herself and walked to her to give her a warm hug. "Close your mouth," she whispered in her ear. "They planned this to surprise us."

"Well, I think they succeeded," Rebecca said quietly. "Why didn't you—"

"Don't blame it on me. I didn't know till we were halfway here and Mom wouldn't let me call or text you to let you know," Olivia defended herself.

Olivia's mother stepped forward. "Hello, Rebecca. It's good to see you again. I know this has been a rough time for Olivia lately and I thought it would do her good to get away for the day.

I spoke with your mother the other evening and she graciously invited us for lunch. It was your mother's idea to keep it a secret from you, too." She laughed lightly. Both the mothers looked very pleased at their scheme's success.

"Thank you for the surprise," Rebecca replied. "Oh, and it's good to see you again, too," she said, remembering her manners.

They moved from the hallway to the kitchen. "Can I help with lunch, Mom?" Rebecca asked.

"I've got everything under control," she assured her. "It's all in the oven. Why don't you and Olivia go to your room to catch up while Eliza and I get to know each other better?" The two mothers sat down at the table with coffee cups and the coffee pot close at hand.

Rebecca grabbed Olivia by the hand and led her to her room. She closed the door behind them then leaned back against it as she pulled Olivia to her for a long kiss. She felt like a nomad roaming through the desert, finally finding water after going without for days. She drank in Olivia's kiss, feeling the heat from her soft lips travel right through her down to her toes. Olivia pressed her firmly back against the door and hungrily intensified the kiss. Tongues danced excitedly and their breathing became short gasps, interwoven with soft moans. The heavy tread of Rebecca's father as he headed down the hallway brought them both back to the reality of their surroundings. Olivia stepped away quickly and, in unison, they began, "I'm sorry, I…" Then both hesitated and began to laugh.

Rebecca grabbed both of Olivia's hands in her own. "I guess I got carried away," she said softly, "but I've been thinking about doing that all week. You look fabulous by the way. It's all I can do to keep from staring at you."

Olivia grinned at this admission. "I'm so glad. As long as you're staring at me, I don't have to worry about someone else catching your eye."

"I'm more worried about making a fool of myself tripping over my tongue 'cause it's hanging down to the floor."

Olivia laughed. "Please don't trip over your tongue." She shot a naughty, sideways glance toward Rebecca. "You might hurt it and I have other plans for it."

"Hmmm," Rebecca pulled her closer again and traced a path up her neck to her ear where she nibbled until she felt Olivia shivering against her. "Was that what you had in mind?"

"That and more," she whispered, seductively. "When I finally get you alone and the time is right, I promise so much more."

"You are determined to bring me to my knees," Rebecca said, feeling them try to buckle at Olivia's words.

"That might not be so bad," Olivia hinted suggestively.

Rebecca stepped past her, knowing she needed to try to put some space between them. With Olivia talking to her and looking at her like that, she wasn't sure she could walk far, so she sat near the door at her desk chair. Olivia sat on the edge of the bed, putting a little physical distance between them but keeping the fire burning, with her eyes tracing Rebecca's breasts and hips as surely as if they were her hands. Her tongue traced her sensual red lips and Rebecca swore she could feel it touching her own lips.

"Stop," Rebecca pleaded. "I'm never going to be able to go back out there and face them if you don't let me get control of myself."

"Oh, all right," Olivia said, taking pity on her. "I just couldn't resist. I don't think you realize how damn sexy you are or what you do to me."

Rebecca would have never thought of her skinny frame and loose-jointed mannerisms as sexy. Certainly none of the guys had ever given her that impression when they looked at her. But with Olivia she was surprised to realize that she did feel sexy. Somehow Olivia made her feel more like a woman and glad to be one.

"I'd like to take a rain check on that promise for more," Rebecca said, smiling suggestively at Olivia.

"Now, you said I had to behave, so you do, too," Olivia complained, laughing. "Tell me about your week instead. Are you ready for your finals?"

They talked about school for a while then Rebecca remembered the conversations she'd had with June and her father. "I need to catch you up on a few things around here,

Olivia," she said, turning the topic from school to home. "I've been having some interesting discussions with some of my family."

"Really?" Olivia was immediately interested. "Can I guess the topic?"

"Probably. On Thanksgiving Day my middle sister June came over in the afternoon and I told her about me…us."

"How did she take it?" Olivia seemed wary of the answer she would hear after her own experiences.

"Pretty good, actually. I really don't think she was that surprised once she allowed herself to think it. That was a lot easier than the one this morning, though."

"Uh-oh, what happened this morning?" Olivia looked as if she were almost afraid to ask.

"Dad and I talked while Mom was at the grocery store. Dad and I don't ever talk about things like feelings, so it was tough. I don't think he really likes the idea of me being a lesbian, but I think he'll be there for me. You know, I've been pretty fortunate overall. God gave me a pretty good family."

"Yes, he did," Olivia said, sounding a little envious.

"Oh, Olivia, I'm sorry. I wasn't trying to compare."

"I know, Rebecca. I'm really happy for you. You are really blessed, you know."

"I'm even more blessed now, after meeting you," Rebecca said, looking across the room into Olivia's eyes.

She rose from the chair and crossed over to sit next to Olivia on the bed, although she knew it was dangerous to her emotional control. She had just touched her lips to Olivia's when she heard her mother call them for lunch. They smiled at each other, their eyes speaking volumes as they rose together and headed out of the room.

When they drew near to the kitchen doorway, the aroma of food grabbed their attention. They sat at the table with their parents and enjoyed the baked chicken with roasted potatoes and vegetables Rebecca's mother had prepared. Dessert was homemade apple pie and vanilla ice cream. Rebecca thought her mother made the best apple pie in the world. Eliza raved about it, confirming her belief.

"How long can you stay?" Rebecca asked.

"Well, I was hoping to have a chance to speak to you two about your detective work," Eliza explained, her gaze taking in both Olivia and Rebecca. "Olivia, I saw your notebook lying open on the table when I was at your apartment last week. I wasn't trying to pry but the notes caught my attention and I realized what it was about. I saw your list of questions and I can answer two of those questions…as soon as we help Beth clean up," she said, noticing Rebecca's mother had started to clear the table.

After much protest, Beth relented to having the help and Rebecca's father escaped with a mischievous smile to the living room as the four women cleaned the kitchen. They sat down around the table afterward, eager to begin the discussion.

Eliza began. "There was something else I was keeping from you, but it was to protect Grandmama to avoid upsetting her more. Your two uncles and I had sworn each other to secrecy but under the circumstances they've given me permission to tell you what happened at Mary Farthing's grave," she continued.

Rebecca was surprised. She had expected to hear about the mysterious phone conversation, not an explanation of the disturbed grave.

"Gran made me promise in the weeks before she died to fulfill a last request for her. You know there was never anyone else in her life after Mary. She grieved for her all those years. Her request was difficult because it had to be done without Grandmama's knowledge because Grandmama would have put a stop to it if she had known. So she enlisted my help. We grew close the last years of her life when we stayed for months at a time with The Greats while your father was deployed, Olivia. I couldn't deny her this request."

The suspense was getting to Olivia, who was wishing her mother would skip the explanations and get to the answers. Her mother recognized her impatience and waved a hand at her. "Okay, I'll get to it. Gran's last request was to be buried beside Mary Farthing. Grandmama had Gran cremated and had her ashes sealed into an urn, which she keeps on her fireplace mantel. Steve, Pat, and I had to figure out how to get the ashes without Grandmama's knowledge. I took her out of town to a crafts festival two months ago while Steve took the urn to the crematorium where a friend of his works. They were able to unseal the urn, place the ashes in a smaller urn and replace Gran's ashes with dust. Grandmama is to never know that the urn she keeps contains only dust."

"Wow!" Olivia said. "I didn't know you could be so sneaky. Aren't you afraid Uncle Steve will let it slip?"

She smiled. "Your uncle is frightened enough of what our mother's reaction would be that I think he may be able to keep this secret. Uncle Pat came into town for business the end of October and on Halloween night we drove here and buried the small urn at Mary's grave. Gran said she missed a lifetime with Mary and didn't want to be separated from her for an eternity. That's why you found freshly overturned dirt at the grave," she said, turning to Rebecca.

"Why did you wait so long?" Olivia asked. "Gran died years ago."

"Grandmama can be a formidable foe," she said, smiling a little sheepishly. "I guess I've gotten a little more brave as I've aged. You know, watching you make the choices you've made in your life has been inspiring to me, Olivia. If you're brave enough to face the prejudice of a whole society, surely I could be brave enough to risk bringing my mother's wrath down upon my head. Your uncles share the blame too, and that helps," she reminded Olivia.

"What about the other questions?" Olivia probed. "We still don't know who Grandmama's father was or the story behind him."

"I'm sorry," Eliza said. "But that's one question we may never be able to answer. Gran may have been the only one who knew the answer and if so she took it with her to her grave."

The women shared their feelings of sorrow over the tale of love lost. Then Eliza reached over to place her hand on Olivia's where it rested on the table. "I believe Grandmama has chosen to ignore the things she disagrees about with you, Olivia. She asked this morning how you were doing, so I know she still cares about you. When I've tried to discuss it, she stops me immediately and says she refuses to have another word said about it. I know it's not acceptance, Olivia, but can you settle for at least a superficial relationship with her for now? Maybe she'll relent with time."

Eliza waited for a response from her daughter, concern evident in her eyes. Rebecca could tell Olivia was struggling to smile, unshed tears threatening to overflow onto her cheeks. "Mom, I love Grandmama so of course I'll take whatever relationship I can get. Just please don't ask me to deny who I am."

Eliza rose from her chair and came around the table to hug her daughter. "I will never do that again, sweetheart," she said, and now the tears did fall.

Beth retrieved a box of tissues from the counter and set it onto the table near them. She sat down again, scooting her chair closer to Rebecca's, and placed one hand on her daughter's shoulder and the other over her hands on the table. She gave her a small squeeze, conveying her love and support through the simple gesture. The other two women regained their composure and dried their tears.

"Well, I guess that signals the end of *Harmon and Wilcox, Private Investigators*," Olivia attempted to joke, but a sniffle still escaped.

Rebecca helped her in her attempt to lighten the mood. "I think we did a pretty good job, considering this was our first case," she said, mockingly boastful. The two mothers quickly joined in the banter, praising the genius of their two daughters.

Another two hours passed with the four women sitting around the table, sharing stories and laughing about the misadventures of Olivia and Rebecca as they grew up. Rebecca blushed several times as her mother found embarrassing stories to tell, but Olivia was able to withstand the teasing better and didn't even turn pink.

Eliza finally, reluctantly, rose to her feet. "I've had a wonderful day," she said. "But I'm afraid it is time to go. Grandmama has probably gotten on Steve's last nerve by now. I promised him I'd return no later than six. Beth, thank you so much for inviting us here."

The others rose as well. Rebecca was suddenly shy in front of her mother and Eliza but managed to return Olivia's quick kiss and strong hug, although her cheeks reddened again. They bade farewell to Rebecca's father as they passed through the living room to the front door. He had been caught up in a Clint Eastwood movie marathon all afternoon. As their visitors drove away, Rebecca turned to her mother, gave her a hug and said, "Thanks, Mom. You're the best."

"I know," her mother responded. "Just remember that tomorrow afternoon."

"Why?" Rebecca asked, suddenly wary. "What's tomorrow?"

"Don't worry, I won't tie up more than three or four hours of your time, but we need to make a huge dent in our Christmas shopping or we will never get it done."

"Christmas?" Rebecca said in an incredulous voice. How had her favorite holiday gotten this close without dominating her attention? Sure, she had noticed the mall decorations and Christmas sales, but she hadn't even asked her mother if she could put the tree up yet. And she hadn't even started thinking about buying gifts.

Wow. Olivia must have me more turned around than I thought.

CHAPTER FIFTEEN

Sunday afternoon found Rebecca riding with her mother to town. She knew her mother didn't love shopping like Aunt Patsy did, but she tolerated it better than Rebecca. They found her dad's gifts first—a six-inch-high replica of his beloved antique tractor for him to place on the mantel, and an antique-tractor calendar for his shop.

Then it was time to find something for Grandma. She was more difficult to shop for, always insisting she needed a new duster and nothing else. All of her children would buy her the same thing and her closet would overflow with new dusters. Rebecca had to admit though, the only day of the week she ever saw her grandmother in anything other than the linen snap-up dresses was on Sunday when she went to church, so maybe it was the perfect gift. She and her mother looked diligently for a different type of gift but inevitably found themselves standing at a small rack of dusters trying to decide which design to choose.

While her mother looked for gifts for June, Kate, and their husbands, Rebecca found herself enjoying the shopping for the youngest member of the family, baby Dean. She spent thirty minutes trying out nearly a whole row of baby toys and her mother laughed to see the sudden regression in her nearly grown daughter. They finally made their selections and Beth stated her satisfaction with the progress they had made.

"Mom?" Rebecca asked. "Can I ask your advice? I, uh, want to get something for Olivia, but I'm not sure what would be—"

Her mother raised her hand to stop her attempted explanation. "I recommend something that takes a lot of thought, but a modest expense. I can see how much she means to you, but you've only known Olivia for a few weeks. She'll be thrilled with the thought you put into a gift, much more so than if you spend a lot of money."

Rebecca realized she couldn't really argue with anything her mother had said. Her work-study job didn't allow for an expensive gift, anyway. "Okay," she told her mother. "I'll think about it."

They stopped by Kate's house before heading home. She was home alone that afternoon, resting for the week of work ahead and catching up on her laundry and housekeeping. Jimmy was at his parents' house, working on his van in their garage. His father and brother were helping pull his blown motor so they could rebuild it. It had been a few weeks since Rebecca had spoken with Kate and she felt a little awkward at first, almost like she was a stranger. She realized then how much she had changed in just a matter of weeks. Kate didn't seem to notice a difference and the opportunity never presented itself for Rebecca to really talk with her.

Their time was mostly spent making plans for Christmas. Kate had to work in the afternoon on Christmas Day, so they agreed to have their Christmas celebration the evening before. They would leave Dad's gifts at Kate's house so he wouldn't find them. Kate would wrap them and bring them with her on Christmas Eve. She and Jimmy would go to his parents Christmas morning—they only lived a few minutes from them, easier to get back and get ready for work. This worked for June, also. They could spend Christmas Eve with her family and Christmas Day with J.T.'s folks. Rebecca realized she hadn't even discussed Christmas with Olivia and wasn't sure if they would be able to meet at all.

On their way home, an advertisement on the radio for a pottery studio gave Rebecca an idea for a gift and her mother agreed it would be a good idea. Rebecca had never been good with arts and crafts but her mother was. She agreed to help her design and make her gift the following weekend.

The final week of classes sped by. Olivia and Rebecca spoke nightly on the phone. They agreed to let go of their mysteries from the past, believing the last of their questions would never be answered. Instead they concentrated on the future. By Wednesday, Rebecca had gathered enough courage to tell Olivia her thoughts for the following school year.

She had picked up information at the community college in Rockford about their main campus only forty-five minutes out of St. Louis. She wanted to be closer to Olivia but wasn't sure if she could afford more than the community college. Rebecca envied Olivia whose paternal grandparents had bequeathed her a large college fund. But she knew she would rather have her Grandma alive and present in her life than a college fund.

"Olivia," she started hesitantly. "I've been thinking about next year, the fall semester you know. I checked things out at the community college's main campus up by St. Louis. I thought about trying to move up there so I could be closer to you."

Olivia started to reply, but Rebecca cut her off. "They don't have dorms but they can help you find affordable housing nearby. I'd only be about forty-five minutes away." She waited nervously.

"Bec, that's great! Maybe we could find a place together, in between our schools," she hesitated slightly, "if you want."

"Really? I mean, are you sure you want me around all the time? You might get tired of me, you know." Rebecca tried to make light of her true concern, that Olivia might not like her as well if she was subjected to her twenty-four/seven.

"I'm sure, Bec. But if you're worried I'll change my mind, it's still, ten months away? I think by then I can convince you."

Olivia's argument made good sense so Rebecca relaxed a

little. "I guess you're right. I'll find a job so I can pay my half of things, though," she insisted.

"I don't suppose you'd consider being my personal masseuse, would you?" Olivia suggested playfully.

Rebecca chuckled deeply. "I think all of those services will be rendered free of charge, Liv. Or maybe we could take it out in trade."

"Ooh, sounds interesting. I can't wait." Olivia's voice became more serious. "What do you think your mom and dad are going to think about it?"

"I don't know. I guess I'll have to find out the hard way. They may fuss a little bit at first, but Mom's been encouraging me to make some decisions about the future so maybe she'll see this as a good start. I've been wondering when to talk to them and I think I'll wait until after the holidays."

"I hope they don't give you a hard time," Olivia replied.

* * *

Friday evening they attempted to figure out their holiday schedules so they could see each other. "Mom and I are flying out to Oregon the day after Christmas." Olivia said. "I was supposed to stay until the tenth of January, but I convinced Mom to let me change my ticket. Now I'm flying back on the third. I thought maybe we could spend some time together that week before classes start again."

Rebecca's heart tripped at the idea of spending an uninterrupted week with Olivia. "At your place, right?" she said hopefully.

"I was hoping most of it would be at my place." Olivia's tone made her intentions clear.

"I'll be there," Rebecca promised. She swallowed and shook her head to clear her mind. "What about before Christmas? I hope I can see you a few times before then."

"When are you finished with finals?"

"My last one is Thursday, the thirteenth. What about you?"

"Ooh," Olivia groaned. "I'm not done until the following Monday."

"Shoot! I was hoping we could get together next weekend."

"Wait!" Olivia nearly shouted. "I just checked my schedule. I have finals on Wednesday, Thursday and then my last one is Monday. I'll be done with most of my studying by Thursday. Maybe I could drive down Saturday morning and head back first thing Sunday morning. That would give me plenty of time to study before Monday's test. What do you think?"

"I think it sounds like a plan. What about the next week or weekend?"

"We're having a family dinner at Grandmama's on the twenty-third. I promised Mom I would help her get ready for it the day before. But maybe between my final on Monday and the weekend we can figure something out. Talk to your parents and see if maybe you can visit me."

"I'll see what I can do. Maybe you can help me convince them next Saturday when you're here." Rebecca knew both her parents liked Olivia and felt her chances would be better with her help. It looked like her holidays were suddenly looking bright.

* * *

Both Rebecca and Olivia hit the books that weekend, preparing for their tests, although Rebecca found time to drive into Rockford with her mother on Saturday morning. They went to the pottery store where Rebecca's mother helped her design and make matching coffee cups for her and Olivia. Her mother had exchanged phone numbers with Eliza the preceding week so Rebecca was able to contact her without going through Olivia. Rebecca had asked Eliza to email her a recent picture of Olivia. She was able to place pictures of Olivia and herself on the cups, with the title *HARMON & WILCOX, P.I.* After adding some artwork her mother thought would fit, she was pleased with the final results. She hoped Olivia would recognize the feelings she had put into her work.

Rebecca watched her mother make the rounds of the pottery store while she waited in line to pay for her finished cups. She saw her stop to look closely at a green vase displayed on a table with various other assorted glass designs. When she noticed her passing by it a second and third time, she made a decision.

Wednesday morning before she went to work, Rebecca took another trip to the pottery store. The price on the green vase was more than she anticipated and it put a significant dent in her checking account, but after all the support her mother had given her the past month, she deserved it. The store gift-wrapped it and Rebecca took it to Kate's house in Rockford for safe keeping until Christmas.

There were six years between Rebecca and Kate and they had never been as close as she and June were. She thought about bringing up some of the recent changes in her life but Kate was in a hurry to get ready for work on the afternoon shift at the nursing home and Rebecca didn't want a rushed discussion.

Thursday afternoon, Rebecca skipped down the hall after finishing her test. She felt good about all of her tests and was pleased with her accomplishments during her first semester of classes. She ran through the cold December air to her Buick and headed home to celebrate. Her mother had promised apple pie again for dessert in honor of her achievements. Along the way, she stopped at a local convenience store for a cherry Coke. Near the checkout counter, she noticed a small display of locally handcrafted bracelets. Most were of a southwestern style with jade and silver on a strip of leather. One caught her eye, a simple silver band with an inscription delicately carved into it. *The courage to love is the courage to live.* She quickly picked it up and placed it on the counter, digging a little deeper into her pocket to pull out the extra cash.

When she reached home, she texted Olivia to let her know her test went well. Olivia didn't return her text until after five, and she was equally optimistic about her success.

After two slices of apple pie, Rebecca helped her mother with the supper dishes. She retreated to her room as soon as they finished so she could call Olivia. They were both excited about meeting on Saturday. When Olivia asked her what they would be doing, Rebecca had a sudden inspiration.

"Just a minute, Olivia. Let me check with Mom." Rebecca hurried to the living room.

"Mom, can Olivia and I help you and Dad put up the Christmas decorations Saturday?" She knew they planned to decorate that weekend but wasn't sure when. She was relieved to see a smile and nod of approval from her mother. "Thanks, Mom!"

"What have you gotten me into, Bec?" Olivia had sudden images of her and Rebecca struggling to lift a reindeer onto the roof.

"Don't worry, Olivia. It'll be great. Dad does the outside lights and lawn ornaments while Mom is in charge of the tree, the Christmas village, the nativity scene, and the best part. She always bakes the day we decorate and we get fresh warm cookies and hot chocolate."

Olivia was amused by Rebecca's childlike enthusiasm. "Sounds like Mom will be pretty busy."

"She delegates a lot. She tells us where she wants things, then she comes back later and makes us fix it if we don't get it right the first time." Rebecca laughed lightly, remembering past experiences with placing the separate figures of the Nativity scene in countless arrangements before her mother was satisfied. "Trust me, it'll be fun."

* * *

Friday evening, Rebecca helped her father check the bulbs on all the exterior lighting and ornaments. Afterward, her call to Olivia was filled with excitement for Saturday. It must have been contagious, with Olivia sounding more and more interested as Rebecca described the assorted lighted wire figures her father had collected over the years. The thought of decorating was almost more exciting to Rebecca than the thought of seeing Olivia again, feeling the rush of heat that always stole through her when their eyes met. Almost, but not quite. By the time their call ended, they were both eager for morning to arrive for more reasons than just decorating.

CHAPTER SIXTEEN

Saturday morning, Rebecca arose early, going outside to finish her chores before breakfast so they would be out of the way when Olivia arrived. She showered and spent a few extra minutes at the mirror before going to the kitchen for coffee, toast and a bowl of cereal.

"Hmm," her mother said, looking around the edge of her paper. "That's right, Olivia should be here in a couple of hours. All I needed for a reminder was to smell your perfume."

Rebecca blushed then became concerned. "What do you mean? It's not too strong, is it?"

"No," her mother laughed. "You smell fine and you look fine. I'm just trying to pay you back for all those times you teased your sisters."

Rebecca filled her coffee cup, buttered her toast then sat down across from her mother. Her mother scanned the paper faithfully every day, looking for any of her "kids" from the school. To her delight, several of the troubled youth she had counseled over the years went on to be recognized in the surrounding communities for their civic efforts. Unfortunately, she also discovered some of their names in arrest reports or even obituaries. Rebecca never scrutinized the paper like her mother did, but sometimes she would scan the headlines on the back of it as her mother read the other side.

"Mom, did you see that article about the centenarians?" she asked.

"The what?" Her mother sounded puzzled, turning to the front of the paper to find the small article Rebecca was referring to, near the bottom corner.

"Local Retirement Community Home to Four Centenarians" headed the article. "That's where Kate works," her mother said. "I guess I skipped that one." She scanned the article briefly then stopped and peered around the paper at her daughter. "Rebecca," she said excitedly. "What was the name of the man you were looking for, the one in that picture?"

"Ralph Dunlop," Rebecca offered. "Why, did you find a Dunlop?"

"I did better than that!" she exclaimed. "I found Ralph Dunlop."

Rebecca called Olivia as she was backing the Buick out of the driveway. "Meet me in Rockford at the courthouse," she said. "I'll explain more then."

Next, she called Kate and asked if she could stop by with a few questions about one of the residents at her job. Kate assured her she would be home and Rebecca pushed the speed limit to get to her house quickly. When she pulled into Kate's driveway, she noticed their car was gone and she found Kate home alone when she entered the house.

"Hey, big sis," Rebecca greeted her. "How've you been?"

Kate gestured to a basket of laundry that was overflowing onto the couch. "Just shove that out of your way and sit down." She returned to the recliner in front of the TV where she had obviously spent most of the morning, judging from an empty plate on the end table beside her, presumably left there after breakfast, an empty coffee cup beside it and a bottle of Coke with a growing condensation ring surrounding it. She certainly hadn't spent any time fixing herself up, judging from the baggy sweatpants and sweatshirt she wore, undoubtedly Jimmy's based on their size. Her hair, usually moussed or gelled into place, was flattened in the back and on one side. Remnants of her makeup from the previous day remained where she had failed to remove it. Rebecca reminded herself that she certainly couldn't be considered fashionable either. Besides Kate worked nights and it was still early.

"Don't be in any hurry to get out of school and get married, kid. Trying to keep up with this house is impossible. Jimmy can be such a slob. Taking care of him is nothing, though, compared to taking care of all those old folks at the home. Sometimes I think if I have to go to work one more day I will just die."

Kate always had been the drama queen of the family. Sometimes Rebecca found it hard to believe they were from the same parents and were raised in the same home.

"So what are you wanting to know, kid?" Kate continued.

"Mom saw an article in the paper about Ralph Dunlop being a centenarian. I was just wondering what you know about him."

"Well, technically I'm not supposed to tell you anything about him, you know. HIPAA rules prevent me from talking. But I guess you won't tell anyone so I can tell you a little."

Rebecca stifled a smile at how quickly her sister's principles would bend if it meant a chance to gossip.

"He's kind of an odd-turned fellow, an old bachelor from what I understand. Never has any family come to visit. Has a lot of nightmares and is really grouchy sometimes. It seems like he's really nice when he first meets you, but the closer you get to him, the meaner he gets. So why do you want to know?"

"Well, do you remember my friend Olivia? You met her at the pizza place a few weeks ago?"

Kate nodded and took a large gulp from her soda while Rebecca continued. "She's been investigating some of her family tree. She has an old picture of her great-grandmother and Ralph is also in the picture. She's trying to find some information about her great-grandfather and I thought maybe he could help."

"He probably could, his memory is pretty good still for his age. But I don't understand how you got involved in all of this. Who is this Olivia, anyway?"

Rebecca knew this was her opportunity to tell Kate everything but she hesitated. Finally, she decided to take the risk and tell all.

"Kate, I've been meaning to talk to you about some things but it just hasn't been the right time. I guess I haven't got an excuse today so here goes."

Kate was looking perplexed but stayed silent, waiting.

"I've been going through some changes lately, Kate. I guess you could say I'm figuring out who I really am."

"Okay, Bec, I'm starting to get confused here. What the hell is going on?"

"Well, I'm trying to tell you. Just give me a minute. All the way through high school, I never had a boyfriend—"

"Yeah, you were always too busy for the guys. I thought you were a little crazy, choosing homework over going out with a good-looking guy, especially that guy Robert who always had the hots for you."

"First of all, Kate, Robert did not have the hots for me. He only wanted to sit close to me so he could copy off my algebra tests. I know why I never dated in high school, Kate. It's because I was never really interested in any of the guys in school."

"What, and now you've met some cool guy in college, right? What does this have to do with Olivia? Is she his sister or something?" Kate moved forward in the recliner, watching Rebecca attentively.

"No, Kate. I haven't met a cool guy in college. I wasn't interested in guys then and I'm still not." She waited a few seconds to see if her words would sink in. "Get it, Kate? I'm not interested in guys. I'm interested in women."

"What?" Kate practically screeched. She waved her arm wildly, pointing an index finger at her. "You are not some freaking lesbian, little sister! I won't have it. I know some of them at work and I know you're not one of *them*."

Rebecca dropped her head, trying to figure out how to explain to her sister. When she looked up again, she was surprised at the contorted expression on Kate's face, somewhere between anger, disbelief and confusion.

"Just think about it, Kate. It all makes sense. I just didn't realize it until now. You know as well as I do that I'm a lot different than you and June. Try to picture me married to some good-old boy with a baby on my hip. It's not for me, Kate. That's not who I am."

"I can't picture you with a woman either, kid. Just the thought of seeing you kiss another woman turns my stomach." Kate gagged for effect. "And what about Mom and Dad? You better never tell them. This is going to kill them."

"They already know…and so does June."

"What?" she screeched again, this time throwing both hands up in the air. "Why didn't someone tell *me*? Why am I always the last to know anything?" She stood up and paced the room, her frustration at being left out evident.

Rebecca was finding it hard to keep up with her sister's rapidly changing emotions. "Don't be mad at them, Kate. They were waiting for me to talk to you first. I asked them to wait. I didn't mean to upset you but I wanted a chance to try to explain things to you."

"Well, you did upset me. And, for the record, I think you're making a big mistake. You'll look back on this someday and think, I should have listened to Kate." She emphasized her words by shaking her finger at Rebecca again. "So, what, is this Olivia your girlfriend or something?"

Rebecca still felt a slight blush in her cheeks at the thought of having a girlfriend but nodded her confirmation.

"I never would've guessed her to be a freak."

Rebecca flinched at her sister's words but Kate didn't seem to notice.

"Well, I hope you don't get burned too bad, little sister. Just remember, I warned you. Don't come crying to me when you get your ass kicked for being a dyke. Stupid damn dykes," she muttered.

"Kate, can you at least be civil to Olivia and me when you see us?" Rebecca was developing a slow burn at Kate's comments. She could handle her disagreeing with her choices, but now she was just being rude. She hoped Kate wouldn't continue her behavior every time she saw her, especially in front of Olivia.

"Of course. What do you think? I have manners, you know. I'll put on my little act like everything is okay but you'll know what I really think." She flopped down into the recliner again, apparently exhausted from her tirade.

Rebecca strived to remain civil. "Kate, I'm really sorry you feel this way. I guess I should have expected someone to take it badly. Thanks for the info about Dunlop. I gotta go now and meet Olivia. Guess I'll see you at Christmas."

Rebecca stood abruptly and turned her back on her sister, struggling to keep a lid on her anger, trying to keep it together long enough to get out the door.

"Yeah, see you at Christmas." Kate didn't even get up as Rebecca walked out.

Rebecca let her anger boil over as she walked and she slammed her fist down on the roof of the car. She backed out of the driveway spinning gravel under her tires.

It would be another quarter hour before Olivia was due to arrive so she drove to the courthouse where they were to meet then took a brisk walk around the grounds of the historic old building to cool down. By the time she saw Olivia's little import car at the stop sign a block away, she was able to turn her thoughts back to Ralph Dunlop and Olivia.

As soon as Olivia pulled her Kia to a stop, Rebecca tapped the window of her passenger door. Rebecca quickly climbed inside, the newspaper in hand.

"You're never going to believe who Mom found in the paper!"

She showed Olivia the article and watched her scan it quickly, seeing her eyes stop when she reached Ralph's name. "Oh…my…Is this our Ralph?" She crumpled the paper as she waved it around in her excitement.

Rebecca smiled and nodded. "And he lives right here in Rockford."

A buckled seat belt impeded her movements but she awkwardly embraced Rebecca with the paper still in one hand.

As soon as Rebecca could free herself from Olivia's excited hug, she rescued her mother's newspaper then buckled her seatbelt. "Let's go!"

Olivia looked momentarily puzzled. "Let's go to the nursing home," Rebecca said. "I want to talk to Ralph Dunlop, don't you?"

"Show me the way!" Olivia said as she backed out of the parking spot.

A few minutes later Rebecca and Olivia entered the nursing home and quickly found the hallway with room 207 where Kate had said Ralph Dunlop would be. "Do you think we should check with the nurses before we go to see him?" Olivia asked in a concerned voice.

"I guess that might not be a bad idea," Rebecca agreed. "He might not feel good today or something."

They stopped at the nurses' desk and spoke with the 200-hall charge nurse. Rebecca broke one of her own rules and made up a white lie, telling the nurse that Olivia was a cousin of Ralph's and hadn't seen him in years, but had seen his name in the paper and came by to visit. The nurse assured them that Ralph liked to visit with people and pointed them down the hall toward his room. Rebecca headed down the hall with Olivia, trying to think of what she'd said to the nurse as a necessary lie.

They knocked loudly on the closed door of room 207 and waited. A deep, gravelly voice beckoned them. "Come in."

In the dim light of the room they saw a bent, frail, gray-haired man sitting in a wheelchair by a hospital bed. The light from his TV, alive with an episode of *Bonanza*, brightened the room but the drapes were closed and the fluorescent lights over the beds were off.

The hospital bed closest to the door was turned sideways against the left wall of the room and that half of the room appeared unoccupied, with no personal effects on the bedside table or end table. Ralph apparently resided on the far side of the room. A few old pictures of a younger man decorated the walls, one with a team of horses, one with a rusty old Farmall tractor, and one with a Ford truck.

Olivia spoke first. "Mr. Dunlop, my name is Olivia Harmon and this is my friend, Rebecca Wilcox. We recognized your name in the newspaper article about the centenarians and wondered if we might ask you a few questions?"

He didn't seem surprised at her explanation and had probably answered many questions before about his one hundred years of life and his experiences. "Please turn the light on over that other bed so I can see you better," he requested.

Rebecca stepped across the room and pulled the small chain leading to the light, illuminating the man's craggy face. Several notches were hollowed out on his nose, cheekbones and ears, from skin cancers being removed, she assumed.

"I'm a little hard of hearing so I'm afraid you'll have to speak up." He spoke louder than necessary. "Now what did you say your names were?"

Olivia repeated their names, this time a few decibels louder. He nodded that he had heard and she continued. "I saw your name in an old photo album of my great-grandmother's."

He looked surprised at this and asked, "Just who was your great-grandmother?"

Olivia said, "Jane Smith, or, actually, I guess it was MJ Farthing."

Neither was prepared for his reaction.

The old man dropped his head into his hands and began to sob loudly. Rebecca and Olivia looked around the room nervously, unsure how to respond or proceed. Finally, Olivia walked over and sat down on the bed beside his chair. She placed an arm over his bent shoulders and began to shush him quietly as one would do with an upset child. Rebecca took a seat in the only chair in the room, next to the TV, and intently watched the scene unfold.

After several minutes of sobbing, he lifted his head and his voice croaked out as he told Olivia, "I don't deserve your kindness, you don't understand." Then he dropped his head down again, but this time the sobs were quieter and more controlled.

Five long minutes elapsed before he lifted his head again. Rebecca arose and handed him some tissues from a nearby bedside table and he wiped his eyes then blew his nose. He looked sadly at both girls then shook his head.

"I can't believe she kept a picture of me after everything that happened. I thought I would be the last person she would want to remember. Is MJ still living?" he asked with a flicker of hope in his old eyes.

"No." Rebecca was the first to speak. "Jane died several years ago." She paused a moment to allow him to absorb this information before continuing. "We thought you would have known that Mary, MJ, died in February of nineteen thirty-three."

"No, I didn't know," he admitted, his shoulders drooping a little further with the news. "When I left, I was so ashamed of myself that I never looked back. I didn't want to be reminded of the person I really was."

Rebecca was becoming very curious about Ralph's story, but she reminded herself that she had questions that still needed to be answered about the identity of Grandmama's father before she allowed herself to become distracted by other questions.

"But why did you girls say you were here today?" Ralph asked.

Olivia responded this time. "Gran, um, Jane didn't talk a lot about that time period. After Mary died, she just kind of went into a shell. She even had a hard time opening up to her daughter...well, actually, Mary's daughter, but Gran raised her as her own. We thought maybe you could give us some information that could answer some questions we have."

"You know, I was a few years younger than Mary, but I knew her for several years even before she moved to the city," he began. Then he jerked in the chair as if he'd been slapped, causing both Rebecca and Olivia to sit up straighter and look at him with concern. "Wait, I thought you said Mary died in February, nineteen thirty-three. Did you say she had a daughter?"

"Yes," Olivia confirmed. "That was one of the things we wanted to ask about—"

Ralph interrupted her before she could continue. "When? When did she have this daughter?"

Rebecca was becoming more concerned about the man's actions, afraid his frail frame couldn't withstand his increasing excitement.

Olivia answered with the date of her Grandmama's birth, "February third, nineteen thirty-three."

Ralph grew quiet for a moment, nodded, then suddenly asked harshly, "And when did you say Mary died?"

"The same day. She died during childbirth."

Olivia's words were quiet, but there was no doubt the old man heard her. Rebecca thought her worst fears had been confirmed about his physical condition when a loud groan escaped from deep within him. His head dropped to his hands again and he rocked back and forth, alternating between loud sobs and moans. She looked at Olivia then at the door, asking with her eyes if she should get help. Olivia shook her head then reached out to hold the wrinkled, shaking figure in the wheelchair, an arm over his shoulders and the other hand resting on his upper arm closest to her.

He allowed her to comfort him for a while then shrugged her off angrily as his mood suddenly switched. "I don't deserve your kindness," he said gruffly. "Don't you get it?" He looked at the two girls as if they were daft, expecting them to understand what was tormenting him.

"I killed Mary. I killed my beloved Mary!" He dropped his head and began rocking again.

Rebecca and Olivia exchanged confused glances. Rebecca ventured, "Your *beloved* Mary? But Mr. Dunlop, she died in childbirth."

"Yes! I understand that perfectly!" he nearly shouted as he looked up at her, anger sparking from his eyes. "But she would have never died if I hadn't gotten her pregnant."

"Wow," Rebecca said under her breath and leaned back suddenly in her chair. She looked over at Olivia and her concern switched from the old man to the beautiful young woman sitting beside him. Olivia was as white as a sheet and suddenly looked as frail as the man who had just revealed himself to be her great-grandfather.

Ralph had dropped his head again and took several minutes to compose himself. Olivia stayed silent and gradually a hint of color began to return to her face. Rebecca had momentarily been afraid both of them would faint to the floor. This had definitely been a turn in the story neither had anticipated.

Ralph began talking again without looking up. "I loved Mary for years," he said. "I waited for her to come back from St. Louis, to come back to me. Sure I was a few years younger than her, but I was ready to marry and have a family. I thought after all those years in the city she'd be ready to move home and start a family, too. But when she came back she wasn't the Mary who had left. She was MJ. And MJ was never alone." His voice had changed to a mocking tone. "She always had that nosy friend Jane with her. I never had a chance to talk to her and tell her how I felt."

He paused to blow his nose again then continued in an excited, accusatory tone. "I caught them, you know. I caught them in the barn." His voice started out soft but gradually rose in volume. "Jane and Mary were in one of the stalls when I walked in to get some tack for the team. They were kissing and I saw it. It just wasn't natural, you see, and I couldn't believe Mary…my Mary, would do such a perverted thing. That witch Jane must have brainwashed her, put evil thoughts in her head."

He looked at both girls as if expecting them to agree with him, but received only shocked looks in return. He continued in a quieter tone. "When they realized I'd seen them, Mary sent Jane to the house. She didn't want to go, but Mary told her it would be okay."

He looked at each of them again, desperate for understanding, but both girls were still struggling to control their distaste for him and his hateful words. He dropped his head again and continued to plead his case. "I was so angry with her. You have to understand. She took all my dreams and just threw them all away. And for what…a woman? A perverted witch? I told her how I wanted to marry her. She told me it wasn't possible, she loved Jane. I tried to make her understand. I told her it was sick, what she and Jane had, that Jane had bewitched her somehow. And she slapped me. I was so angry."

He looked up at Olivia. "I would have never hurt her, you know. But something inside me must have snapped. It was like it wasn't even me anymore, like I was watching from a distance. I grabbed her and shoved her down into the floor of the stall, and, and…"

Tears began to run down his wrinkled face but he didn't bother to brush them away. He turned to stare at the wall above the television as if no longer aware of his two visitors but trapped in his own nightmare from decades before. "I had my way with her. She tried to stop me, begged me to stop, said if I really loved her I would stop. But I didn't. She should have been with me, not that woman. She was mine."

Rebecca looked at Olivia and tears were streaming down her face as well. She was surprised when she felt wetness on her own cheeks. She felt disgust for this man who was sharing his confession and shame with them. She felt pain for MJ and Jane.

"I left that day. I ran from the barn, leaving Mary crying in that stall. I grabbed my gear and left like the devil was after me. And maybe he was. I've never loved anyone else all these years. My heart belonged to Mary and only Mary, and she broke it. Worse than that, she made me hurt her. I couldn't bear the thought of ever hurting someone else the way I hurt Mary."

His tears stopped at the same time as his words. His face took on an oddly calm expression, as if he had purged his soul of evil and was at peace, finally. The small room was silent for a few minutes and both girls were able to get their emotions under control as they sat quietly, absorbing the effects of his words.

"Well, girls," he said, as he appeared to snap back to the present and become aware of their presence again. "You probably didn't expect a confession from a horrible old man, but that's what you got. I raped Mary Farthing the first week of May, nine months before your grandmother was born."

He spoke harshly and the words sounded surreal to Olivia. She had understood everything he had told her, but the fact she was sitting beside her own great-grandfather and he was admitting to being a rapist was all too much for her.

He tried to place his hand over Olivia's hand on the bed beside her but she withdrew it as soon as he touched her. He nodded slightly as if he had expected this. "Young lady, I'm your great-grandfather and I'm sorry you didn't have one you could respect or care about."

Panicked when he touched her, Olivia's panic was quickly replaced by a look of disgust, then a deep nausea. She leapt to her feet, rushed into the small bathroom and slammed the door.

Rebecca could hear her heaves. She opened the door and stepped into the small room. Olivia was standing upright wiping her mouth with a tissue, and when Rebecca started to give her a hug she gently but firmly pushed Rebecca's arm away.

"I'll be okay." She spoke without tears. "I've got to go back out there, Rebecca. I've got to finish this now, because I may never be able to make myself come back again."

She pushed past her and stepped back into the room with Rebecca right behind her. Olivia returned to sit on the edge of the bed with a little more distance between her and the crumpled man in the chair. Rebecca sat on the edge of her chair, ready to intervene if she saw Olivia getting too upset.

Ralph seemed relieved when she returned. "I know you'll never forgive me," he said. "I've never forgiven myself, either. Thank you for letting me tell someone before I'm gone. I've wanted to confess this so many times over the years, but I've always kept it buried under my shame. Now maybe I can die in peace."

Olivia reached out cautiously and placed one hand on his forearm where it rested on the wheelchair armrest. She chose her words carefully. "I need to think about everything you've told me. I can't promise, but I believe I will be able to forgive you. At least I'm going to try. That's something I need to do for my own peace of mind, not for you, Mr. Dunlop. Thank you for telling me the truth. You're right, it needed to be told. It's a secret that has caused generations of pain and maybe now that it's coming out, some of that pain can be healed."

He nodded and then dismissed them with a gesture. "Please send in a nurse when you leave. I think I need to lie down and rest for a while." He turned to stare at the bed, only he knowing what he was seeing.

As they stepped into the hall, Rebecca gripped Olivia's hand firmly in her own to share her strength with her shaken friend. She could feel the slight tremble that coursed through Olivia's body as they walked and Olivia followed her lead blindly as they walked to the nurses' station and reported Mr. Dunlop's request for a nurse then headed out to the car. Rebecca didn't release Olivia's hand until she had helped her into the passenger seat of the car.

Rebecca asked for her keys and Olivia numbly handed them to her, accepting without argument that Rebecca would drive. She remained quiet on the ride back to the courthouse and Rebecca did not try to interrupt her thoughts. Rebecca sat quietly for several minutes after pulling to a stop beside her Buick and turning off the ignition.

The coldness of the day was beginning to seep into the vehicle before Olivia finally said, "I don't know what to do. It makes me sick to think of how he hurt her. But, in a way, he didn't just end Mary's life, he ended his own. I know he's still here, and one hundred years old, but his life has been wasted. Gran's life was, too, from what Mom says. Three lives ruined by one man in a fit of rage and violence. And the ripples from that one act have affected every generation since then."

Olivia paused to reflect on what she had said. "I need to go back to St. Louis. I need to talk to my mother. You understand, don't you, Bec?" she said, as tears welled in her eyes again. "Thank you for being here with me and for me, but I really need to talk to my mother, in person."

"Of course, I understand," Rebecca said, brushing away a tear from Olivia's cheek. "Would you object if I went along to drive? I can see how upset you are and I don't think it's safe for you to drive two hours on the interstate right now."

"You're probably right," Olivia admitted. "I can bring you back in a day or two. Do you think your mother will mind?"

"I know she won't. She'd probably be pretty upset with me if I didn't insist on making sure you got back in one piece. But I'll call and let her know."

Rebecca quickly called her mother and explained the situation briefly, promising to tell her more, later. She arranged for her mother and her father to come into Rockford later that evening and drive the Buick home for her.

Then she carefully steered Olivia's car through the narrow streets of Rockford and out to the interstate highway, headed for St. Louis.

CHAPTER SEVENTEEN

Olivia called her mother and they agreed to meet at Grandmama's house. Her mother had assured her that Grandmama would be napping for an hour or two around the time they were due to arrive, which should leave them plenty of time to talk. Olivia knew Eliza could hear in her voice how upset she was, but Olivia wouldn't share the reason over the phone. The fact that Rebecca was driving her back to St. Louis was another indication of her upset and its seriousness.

Eliza met them at the front door of Grandmama's large house and quickly brought them inside, took their coats and led them to the living room. She gestured for Rebecca to sit in a large high-backed chair and she sat on the sofa, patting the cushion beside her for Olivia. "What's happened to upset you so much?" she demanded.

Olivia haltingly repeated the story they had heard only hours before. Her voice became very low at times as she reported with obvious difficulty the act of violence. If Rebecca hadn't already known the story, she wasn't sure she would have been able to hear her five feet away. Rebecca brought her a box of tissues. Finally, Olivia looked up from her lap where her eyes had remained fastened throughout the telling. She saw the tears on her mother's cheeks where they rolled downward, unchecked.

Olivia hugged her mother tightly and they cried softly together. Rebecca watched from the chair, trying not to cry with them but failing. From her position in the high-backed chair she could not see the doorway from the living room where the hallway led to the rest of the house, but she could sense another presence had entered the room. Before she could say anything, she heard the strong voice of a woman saying, "What is this? What is Olivia doing here and why are you both crying?"

Rebecca wasn't sure whether to run for the door or hide under the chair. She was sure the voice belonged to Grandmama, and she was equally sure she, the *female country bumpkin from a hick town who didn't know right from wrong*, would not be welcome in her house. She opted to sink back into the chair, hoping to remain unnoticed for as long as possible.

This tactic worked only momentarily as Grandmama stepped forward and came around the front of the couch. Her ramrod-straight back and stern features only heightened Rebecca's fear she would soon be ousted. When she saw Rebecca, her steely eyes narrowed. "Who is this?" she demanded, her hands fisted on her hips.

Olivia jumped to her feet to stand between them as if to protect Rebecca. "Grandmama, this is Rebecca, my friend from Springtown. She was kind enough to drive me home when I was too upset to drive myself."

"This is that Springtown woman? I thought I made it clear to you what I thought about you carrying on with her!"

Rebecca could tell she was just getting wound up and she rose to leave before the situation worsened.

"Rebecca, sit down," Olivia ordered in a voice even more stern than her Grandmama's. "And Grandmama, stop it. You had your chance to say how you feel, now it's my turn."

Rebecca sat and Olivia's grandmother stepped backward, obviously surprised by the tone her granddaughter had taken with her. Olivia continued in the same commanding tone, "I will not allow this hatred, this refusal to try to understand, I will not allow it to ruin any more lives."

She continued before anyone could interrupt. "Grandmama, I know you had it rough growing up because of the way people whispered about Gran. She was raising a fatherless child after engaging in a scandalous relationship with another woman. And Gran was withdrawn and distant and didn't support you as well as she should have when you were in pain. But, what you don't know is why. Do you know how MJ ended up pregnant? Because of hatred, hatred for the love Gran and she had for each other. She was raped, Grandmama. Ralph Dunlop, the Farthings' farmhand, raped her after he caught her and Gran kissing in the barn. That was why MJ was pregnant. When MJ died giving birth to you, Gran felt eternally guilty for not being there to stop him. MJ sent her into the house and she went, leaving her out in the barn with Ralph. Ralph hated their love so much, he reacted with violence and hatred. He ruined his life, MJ's life and Gran's life." She said the final sentence with a flat voice, all of the emotion drained from her.

Grandmama slumped to sit on the sofa on the other side of her daughter. Olivia moved over to kneel in front of her. She grabbed both of her hands in her own and looked up into her eyes. "Don't you think it's time to quit hating, before we ruin any more lives? Your childhood was made unbearable at times and now hatred has damaged my relationship with you. Can't you let go of the hatred, Grandmama…for me?"

Grandmama had such a stricken look on her face it was clear that a physical blow could not have impacted her more than her granddaughter's words. Although she opened her mouth to speak, she was unable to respond.

"I love you, Grandmama. Why can't you love me?" Olivia sobbed and put her head down in Grandmama's lap.

Grandmama gently stroked Olivia's hair from her tear-streaked face. "Oh, Olivia," she soothed her granddaughter. "I love you, I do. I've never stopped loving you."

She urged Olivia up onto the couch between her and Eliza and hugged her fiercely to her. Eliza reached around to hug them both from the other side of Olivia. The three generations of women sat together sharing their sorrow and their tears.

Finally, Grandmama released her granddaughter and dried her eyes. "Now let me be sure I understand what you just told me, Olivia. Tell me what you know and how you know it."

Olivia explained to Grandmama how she and Rebecca had been investigating the picture from Gran's photo album. For her mother's sake she carefully omitted the part about the urn buried at the cemetery. She told her of the events of the preceding weeks, finishing with the meeting that morning with Ralph Dunlop and his confession to them. Grandmama looked anguished when she repeated what he had told her about his attack on Mary.

"Your Gran mentioned a few things that finally make sense, now that I know the whole story." She frowned as she returned in her mind to some very painful times in her childhood. "I always thought Gran resented me because I lived and MJ, my birth mother, died. She cried herself to sleep nearly every night. I could hear her through the walls. One night I stopped outside her closed door and I heard her saying over and over again, 'I never should have left her. Why didn't I stay?' I thought at the time maybe they had argued and been separated for some time, possibly when MJ got pregnant. I figured Gran had stepped back in when MJ was due to give birth to a child out of wedlock, with little means of support. Instead, she must have felt guilty all of those years for leaving Mary that day in the barn."

"Gran felt bad that she wasn't there for you when you needed her," Eliza explained. "She told me she hadn't been a good mother, and that she regretted not trying harder. She made me promise to be a better mother than she had been."

"Thank you for that, Eliza. I'm glad the two of you were close in the years before she passed. This is a lot to take in, dear. I always thought when I was growing up that things would be better if only I had a father. Now I find out I do have a father, but I don't believe I will ever be able to forgive him. You are right, you know. He destroyed Mother's life...Jane, that is. I wonder if I was a reminder to her all those years of what happened to

Mary, what might have been different if she'd never left her alone."

Eliza spoke firmly in response. "Mother, you cannot think that. Gran spoke to me of her love for you every day. She felt as much guilt about not being there for you as she did about not being there for MJ. But, who's to say what Ralph might have done if she had stayed. He was out of his head. He could have killed her, or both of them for that matter. We can't go back and second guess. What we can do, though, is make sure we don't make the same mistakes. Olivia is a lesbian. It's not been easy for her. For her life to be happy, she needs our support, not our hatred."

Olivia had let her gaze drop to her lap as her mother spoke. Grandmama reached a trembling hand out and placed a finger beneath Olivia's chin, urging her gently to lift her head. When she could meet her gaze with her own, she held her in place while she said, "Olivia, I am sorry. Your mother is right. I had no right to denounce your friend or your lifestyle. I hope you can forgive a mean old woman."

Olivia blinked hard and sniffled, then replied. "I forgive you, Grandmama, and I'm sorry I'm not the granddaughter you had hoped for."

"Nonsense," was the immediate response. "You are everything I want in a granddaughter."

Rebecca was beginning to feel a little awkward, as if she were intruding upon a private family moment. Olivia must have sensed her growing unease because she stood and walked to her, pulled her to her feet and hugged her, resting her head on Rebecca's shoulder and including her in the emotional atmosphere of the living room.

Rebecca could feel the strength returning to Olivia as she stood holding her. The events of the day had shaken her, but the love of her grandmother had helped her to steady herself and rebuild. She was relieved to see a tentative smile on Olivia's face when she released her.

Grandmama and Eliza had composed themselves as well. Grandmama addressed Rebecca next. "Young lady, maybe I have been hasty in my assessment of you. I apologize for not giving you a chance. You obviously mean a lot to my granddaughter, therefore I will do my best to give you a chance to prove yourself."

Rebecca wasn't totally at ease after this apology and felt she would have to be on her best behavior around Grandmama. She wondered what *proving herself* would involve.

"Now," Grandmama continued, with a sudden change of tone, "I think we've had enough tears for today." She stood up quickly, wiping her eyes one last time to emphasize her point. "I'm hungry. Let's go to the kitchen and see if we can find some ice cream."

Eliza started to protest, but Grandmama stopped her with a look. Rebecca understood immediately where Olivia had learned that determined look.

"The doctors be damned!" Grandmama exclaimed. "I will eat ice cream with my granddaughter if I take a mind to do so!" She turned and strode from the room.

Eliza and Olivia looked at each other, shrugged in unison, then turned to follow. Rebecca brought up the rear, laughing softly to herself.

CHAPTER EIGHTEEN

Rebecca and Olivia stayed for dinner that evening and left shortly afterward. Fatigue from the emotional day was becoming evident in Grandmama's eyes and the others were tired as well. While Olivia drove them toward her apartment, Rebecca called her mother.

"Hey, Mom," she responded when Beth answered the phone. "Thought I'd better call and catch you up on all that's happened."

"I'm glad you called. Your father and I have been worried. We just got back from Rockford with your car."

Rebecca was immediately remorseful for causing the concern that was so obvious in her mother's voice. "Thanks for getting the Buick. I'm staying at Olivia's apartment tonight and Olivia will drive me home tomorrow or Monday after her final."

"We're just glad you made it there in one piece. Next time shoot us a text to let us know you made it," Beth chided gently.

"Sorry. I'll try to remember. I guess you're probably wondering what happened today. I promise we'll give you all the details when we're there. For tonight, can I just give you the short version?"

"Sure."

"We found Ralph Dunlop and he told us he had raped Mary Farthing. He is Olivia's great-grandfather." Rebecca didn't miss Olivia's quick glance in her direction. The pain and sorrow the old man had caused leapt into her eyes anew at the mention of his name.

Beth gasped at the news. "Oh no! How devastating for Olivia!"

"Yeah. That's why I needed to drive her back to the city. She confronted her grandmother with what she had learned and pretty much insisted that Grandmama stop the cycle of hate he started. I think Olivia got through to her. We just left her house and she gave me a good-bye hug." Rebecca had been shocked when Grandmama had approached her and very stiffly placed her hands on her shoulders and leaned toward her. They had nearly touched cheeks together, but Grandmama had carefully retained a thin but definite boundary around herself.

"Good. That sounds promising. Tell Olivia I'm so happy she's made up with her grandmother." Beth sounded sincerely pleased with the news.

Rebecca repeated the words to Olivia.

"Thanks, Mom," Olivia yelled toward the phone.

Beth cleared her throat then spoke softly to her daughter. "Rebecca, I'm not trying to pry and I know you're old enough to make your own decisions, but are you okay with staying the night at Olivia's? We can come get you if you're not."

Rebecca drew down her eyebrows in confusion, struggling to understand. "Of course I'm okay. Why wouldn't I be?"

"Well, you know, you two haven't known each other long and now you're staying the night together…alone…You know I always hoped my daughters would marry before…"

Rebecca understood in a flash and her face burned as she realized what her mother was saying. She realized just as quickly that she absolutely did not want to have this conversation with her mother, especially with Olivia sitting less than a foot away from her. She had the sudden urge to drop the phone and roll down the window for a blast of cold winter air. Instead she swallowed audibly and managed to force out a response.

"Mom, I'm fine." *Gotta end this now before it gets worse!* "I'll talk to you tomorrow. Love you both. 'Bye." Eager to break the link to her mother, she barely waited for her mother's good-bye before she ended the call and slipped the phone into her coat pocket.

"What was that about? Is she worried I won't take good care of you?" Olivia teased as she ran her fingernails lightly up and down Rebecca's thigh.

"No," Rebecca replied hastily, grabbing Olivia's hand to still it and stop the wild sensations threatening to overcome her. "It's nothing. Just Mom being Mom." She hoped Olivia would let it drop and mercifully she did.

When they reached the apartment, Rebecca entered behind Olivia and was suddenly shy. Her mother's words had reminded her of the potential the evening held. She realized she had mostly given her desire the reins, following her instincts when she was with Olivia. Now she had no reason to stop, no parents coming home, no closing of the park gate. Was she ready for the next step?

While Olivia put their coats on the coat rack, she moved Pooh out of the easy chair and onto the couch. She sat stiffly in the chair, trying to calm her nerves. Pooh had remembered her and left her new spot on the couch to climb into Rebecca's lap. The purring feline found it necessary to move around a lot to keep her ministrations in the best locations under her chin and around her ears as Rebecca absentmindedly petted her. Rebecca's mind was spinning furiously through her dilemma. Throughout high school she had no desire to have sex, so she had felt no qualms about supporting abstinence. In her mind it solved a lot of problems—no unwanted pregnancies, less risk of STD, less chance of a guy only going out with her for one reason if he knew the rules ahead of time. But now, her longings for Olivia left her wanting to break all her own rules. Olivia had been moving about the apartment chatting lightly when she noticed the lack of response from Rebecca. "Are you okay?" she asked.

Rebecca nodded distractedly.

Olivia walked in front of her and studied her closely. "Are you worried?" she lightly teased. "Do you think I brought you to my lair and now I'm going to take advantage of you?" She plucked Pooh from Rebecca's lap and placed her unceremoniously onto the couch. Obviously insulted by the lack of proper attention she was receiving from the two, Pooh immediately hopped down and ran from the room.

Olivia straddled Rebecca's lap, a knee on either side of her hips. She leaned back on Rebecca's knees so she could look directly into her eyes. Olivia smiled impishly. "I promise I won't make you do anything you don't want to do."

Rebecca blushed and tried to drop her eyes, but Olivia placed a finger under her chin and kept their eyes locked. She leaned forward and gently kissed Rebecca. Rebecca, shy at first, soon recovered as passion swept through her, fanned by the soft lips pressing against her own. Olivia allowed her to deepen the kiss initially, then slowly eased away to look again into Rebecca's eyes. "I love you, Bec. I promise I'll do my best to never cause you pain."

Rebecca's eyes were wet as she replied, "I love you, Olivia. I may be shy and a little scared about…about…you know, but I trust you completely or I wouldn't be here. Can we just take our time, though?"

"Of course we can, my love. If you want, I'll sleep on the couch tonight and you can have my bed." Before she could answer, Olivia kissed her gently again then stood and pulled her to her feet.

"How about we just wait and see?" Rebecca said, unsure of herself but unwilling to rule out letting things go further with Olivia.

"That sounds like a good plan." Olivia led her over to a chair at the table and poured each of them a glass of cherry Coke.

She placed the glasses on the table then ducked quickly into the bedroom, returning with her notebook and a pen.

"I'd put this away when we thought we wouldn't be able to find more answers to our questions," she explained.

She sat down beside Rebecca and turned to the page of questions they had compiled. After her surprise visit to Rebecca's house for lunch, she had answered questions three and four about her mother's conversation with Uncle Steve and about Mary's grave being disturbed. Now she added to the notation after question two, about Ralph: *Ralph Dunlop, raped MJ Farthing in May, 1932, resulting in pregnancy and, ultimately, in MJ's death*. For question five, about the father to MJ's child, she wrote simply: *See question #2.*

"I wonder if Mom and my uncles will tell Grandmama about burying Gran's ashes at MJ's grave?" Olivia queried. "She might really let them have it for deceiving her, you know."

"I would guess they'll keep it a secret," Rebecca said, thinking of how intimidating Grandmama had looked when she first saw her.

"You're probably right," Olivia laughed. "Now, only one question remains unanswered," she pointed out. "Is Peacock Cemetery really haunted? How do you think we could go about answering that question?"

"I think only time will tell us the answer to that one," Rebecca stated. "I'm glad we know all the other answers now, but I'm sure sorry it happened the way it did all those years ago."

"Yeah. Me, too."

Rebecca changed the subject, not wanting to start any tears again. "You know, I told Dad how I felt about you."

"Really?" Olivia seemed constantly surprised at how open Rebecca was able to be with her family.

"Yeah. It's kind of odd, because he warned me this lifestyle was a tough row to hoe. I know things have changed a lot in the last two or three decades, but there is still hatred, prejudice and fear out there. It's not going to be easy for either of us at times."

"No, it won't. I've already felt some of that in the few years since I've been out. Is that something that worries you, Bec?"

"Maybe a little. I got my first taste of it this morning before we went to see Ralph."

"Before we went to see him?" Olivia looked puzzled.

"Yeah. On the way to meet you, I stopped to ask Kate about Ralph. She works at the nursing home so I asked her a few questions about him. She asked me why I wanted to know then she started asking questions about who you were. The opportunity was there and I'd wanted to tell her about me, so I did. She didn't exactly take it well."

"Oh, Bec. I'm sorry."

"Don't be. It's really okay. I mean, I should have expected someone would be upset about it. Besides, Kate's kind of crazy anyway. She has the role of the family drama queen all sewed up. She'll be upset until the next thing comes along for her to get in a tizzy about then she'll get over it."

"I wish I could tell you that will be the worst you'll experience but it probably won't be," Olivia told her honestly. "Are you sure this isn't going to be too much for you?"

"I'm sure I won't try to live a life as someone I'm not," she said, confidence in her decision evident in her tone. "Meeting you was the best thing that could have happened to me."

Olivia smiled her funny smile which Rebecca was learning to love. She stood and walked around the corner of the table, closing the notebook on the table between them. She straddled Rebecca's legs and sat on her lap again then wrapped her arms around her neck. "My love, meeting you was the best thing that ever happened to me." This time when she kissed Rebecca, there was no hesitation or shyness in Rebecca's response. She returned the kiss eagerly, burning from the heat of Olivia's lips caressing her own, thrilling to the dance of her tongue with Olivia's.

Rebecca stood and pulled Olivia over to the sofa, never breaking contact between their lips during the brief journey across the room. Olivia sat down on the edge of the sofa and Rebecca slid down to her knees in front of her. She pulled Olivia hard up against her, needing to feel her body against her own.

She slid her hands over Olivia's soft curves, hesitating at her hips then sliding up the side of her body to the swell of her breasts.

Olivia moaned as Rebecca cupped one breast. Rebecca was amazed at the flash of heat that shot through her own body when she gently curled her hand under Olivia's breast, then slid her thumb over the nipple, teasing it to hardness under the soft fabric of her lacy bra.

Olivia traced her jawline with her lips, then moved down to her neck, kissing the hollows at the base of her neck, then tracing a path of fire up to her ear with her tongue. Rebecca was beginning to feel disoriented from the overwhelming sensations coursing through her body and Olivia held her tighter when she felt her begin to sway. She leaned her head back, releasing Rebecca's earlobe from between her teeth and laughed lightly.

"Rebecca, my dear Rebecca," she whispered, seeing the fire raging in her eyes. "I want to make sweet love to you. I want to touch every inch of you with my hands and my lips. But only if you're ready, darling, only if you're ready. There's no reason for us to rush this. I'll wait as long as you want."

Rebecca was nearly lost in the flood of desire coursing through her being, but she recognized the sincerity of Olivia's words and searched for the right words to show Olivia her heart. "If I'm scared, it's because I want this to be perfect for you. I want to make you feel everything that I feel when you look at me, when you touch me, when you kiss me. I'm scared…"

"Shhh," Olivia placed a finger softly against Rebecca's lips then softly cradled her face in her hands. "Oh, Bec. Don't you know you do? You make me feel like…like my heart might explode with joy, like I can't get enough of you."

Rebecca turned her head to kiss Olivia's palm. She traced the fine creases with her tongue, chuckling slightly when Olivia jerked her hand away. Suddenly decisive, she said firmly, "Follow me."

"Why? Where are you taking me?" Olivia's eyes met Rebecca's eyes and dared her.

"You'll see. You trust me, don't you?" She lightly pulled on Olivia's arms and she stood then Rebecca backed her way to the bedroom, never dropping their linked gaze. She saw the desire growing in Olivia as she backed her way toward the bed. When she was only inches from it she stopped.

"May I?" Rebecca whispered, reaching for the top button on Olivia's blouse. She found her fingers nearly useless as she tried to unfasten the buttons by feel, watching Olivia's face intently, enchanted by the changes she saw as her color heightened and her eyes became hazy. After an interminable time, the blouse finally fell open. Rebecca reached behind Olivia and after several seconds of fumbling unfastened her bra.

After a deep breath, she reached for Olivia's blouse and finally moved her eyes lower as she slipped the blouse from her shoulders, looking with wonder at her breasts as she gently pulled the bra down, dropping it on the floor beside her.

Resisting the temptation to lose herself in Olivia's full breasts, she unbuttoned Olivia's jeans, slowly pulled the zipper down, slid them over her hips. Olivia put a hand on her shoulders while she kicked off her shoes and socks then stepped out of her jeans. She stood shyly before Rebecca wearing only lacy white panties. Slowly she slid the panties down over her hips, bending to remove them. When she stood again, Rebecca's eyes were irresistibly drawn to the triangle of tight curls beckoning at the vee of her thighs.

Rebecca's mouth was suddenly dry and she licked her lips before trying to speak. "You are so beautiful," she said with wonder.

"Your turn," Olivia whispered. She pulled the snaps apart on Rebecca's shirt, one loud pop at a time, pausing between each one to smile mischievously at her. Rebecca's excitement was mounting with each one and she shrugged the shirt back off her shoulders as soon as the last snap popped. Olivia reached for the bottom of the T-shirt Rebecca had chosen that morning instead of a bra and slid it slowly over her head, dropping it onto the mounting pile of clothes beside them.

"Beautiful." Olivia gently stroked her tight stomach and up around each breast, running her nails lightly along her skin, making her nipples reach out tautly, begging for contact. She traced a path from her breasts to her navel then reached to unfasten Rebecca's jeans. She had barely begun to unzip them when Rebecca hastily shoved jeans and underwear down over her narrow hips, below her knees. Olivia helped her balance long enough to kick free of all her clothing until Rebecca stood beside her, exposed and vulnerable but unafraid.

"Touch me."

Olivia was pleading with her and she heeded her plea, wrapping her long fingers under both breasts and swirling her thumbs around the soft brown of her nipples, watching in amazement as they tightened under her ministrations, loving the sound of Olivia's low moan of pleasure. The gasp that followed when she encircled a nipple with her lips sent a jolt of excitement to her groin. *Oh, God, I could do this forever.* She moved from one breast to the other, showing no favoritism, thrilling with each moan and gasp of pleasure she created, aware of the growing pressure and wetness between her own legs.

Olivia backed Rebecca slowly toward the bed, not stopping until Rebecca was lying on the plush comforter with Olivia above her. Rebecca marveled at the feel of her soft body moving so sensuously across her own. Her breasts were fuller than Rebecca's and her nipples were larger, calling to Rebecca to touch them as Olivia slid them across her own, teasing her nipples. Olivia brought them to Rebecca's lips briefly, only to move them away again as soon as she touched them with her tongue. Olivia moved randomly over her, tasting Rebecca's cheek, her neck, the work-hardened muscles of her arm, the smooth white skin of her stomach.

When Olivia began concentrating her attention around her breasts, Rebecca arched her back to reach her nipples skyward, aching for Olivia to touch them, not knowing until now how such a need could consume her. When Olivia did touch her teasingly with the tip of her tongue, she groaned in ecstasy. She wove her fingers through Olivia's hair, holding her closer to her breast. "Please," was all she could manage.

Olivia answered her call and caught her nipple lightly between her teeth before sucking it into her mouth. She moved to the other breast and the sensations were even more intense. Shock waves of pleasure shooting from her nipples directly to her groin made it hard to breathe and Rebecca no longer could distinguish one pleasure point from the other, only knowing she wanted…no, *needed* more.

When Olivia suddenly released her swollen nipple, she would have cried out but her attention was immediately drawn to the feel of Olivia's fingertips sliding up her thigh and brushing briefly across coarse curls before moving down the other thigh, then back again. Each time her touch became bolder and Rebecca strained toward her more, knowing instinctively she sought that touch. When at last Olivia's fingers found her, she inhaled sharply and held her breath, nearly unable to bear the sweet agony of her touch.

As she stroked her slowly, Rebecca became lost in sensation. Her soft moans of pleasure quickened and Rebecca's body tightened as she rose up to meet her. Olivia slid two fingers into the beckoning wetness and gasped as her lover clamped onto her. "Oh, God. So wonderful." She matched the thrusts of Rebecca's hips. "Rebecca, come for me," she whispered softly, watching her reach that peak, taking her over the edge with a roll of her thumb over her already engorged clitoris, drinking in her cries as she brought her lips to meet Rebecca's.

* * *

Rebecca's arms and limbs felt like they would no longer respond to her commands. She lay unmoving in Olivia's arms, aware that it had been several seconds since she had last breathed, she felt no need to breathe. "You're magic," she whispered in Olivia's ear.

Olivia chuckled. "I don't think it was magic, silly."

Rebecca turned her head to look at Olivia. The relaxed smile, the hair slightly mussed from her hands, that perfect nose, those sparkling green eyes, had to be magic. Even though she had believed her body to be paralyzed after her orgasm swept through her, she felt a streak of excitement shoot straight to her center when her gaze settled on Olivia's soft, lovely lips. She tentatively lifted a hand, pleased to see that her arm did still function properly, and traced those beautiful lips with her index finger. Olivia gently took her finger between her teeth, teasing the tip with her tongue.

The need to touch Olivia, to feel her skin, to explore her body grew stronger as her strength returned. She rolled to her side, content at first to trace her features then caress the planes and valleys of her body, slowly and lightly. She heard the quickening of Olivia's breath as she brushed across her breasts, noticed the twitch of her hips as she crossed her lower abdomen. She wanted to give Olivia the same pleasure she had so unselfishly given her.

"Do you know how sexy you are?" she asked Olivia.

"Thought you said it was magic," Olivia teased, her voice slightly breathless as Rebecca caressed again just above the curls at the vee of her thighs.

"Hmm. Sexy magic," Rebecca agreed. One hand was no longer enough. She pushed herself up from the bed and swung a leg over Olivia, kneeling over her hips. Now she could use both hands to explore. *Much better.* She ran her hands around and under Olivia's breasts, cupping them so she could tease first one then the other nipple with her tongue. When she gently sucked a nipple into her mouth she felt Olivia's pleasure as sharply as if it were her own, as she arched toward her and ran a hand through her hair, pulling her closer. *Heavenly.*

She moved up to kiss those fabulous lips and was surprised by the hunger Olivia could no longer hide from her. Olivia returned her kiss fiercely, devouring her lips and dipping her tongue inside to entice Rebecca's to engage in a frantic dance of desire. Remembering Olivia's excitement earlier, she realized Olivia had put her own desires, her own fulfillment on hold to give her pleasure, to make her first time perfect. Her heart swelled with love for Olivia and she vowed she would never take her for granted.

Rebecca ran her hands down Olivia's body as she moved her lips along the line of her jaw to her ear, down along her neck and biting lightly the sensitive skin she had found along her pulse. When her hand reached the bend of Olivia's thigh, she traced the line inward slowly, feeling Olivia moving her hips in search of her touch. She heard herself gasp when her fingers encountered the wet satin heat between Olivia's legs.

"Oh, Rebecca, yes," Olivia moaned, urging her on.

Rebecca gently slid her fingers deeper and Olivia raised her hips to take her inside. She followed Olivia's lead, moving as Olivia had done with her. Suddenly Olivia's hands were in her hair, pulling her to her as she cried out her name. Rebecca marveled as she felt Olivia's body, shaking and rigid, suddenly melt under her.

Rebecca felt energized, on top of the world. She carefully rolled to her side beside Olivia and gazed at her spent lover tenderly. She placed one hand on her stomach, just to touch her, to feel her skin, and placed her head on Olivia's shoulder. Her mind was alive with wonder at all she had experienced and her heart was still beating fast from the excitement of their lovemaking, yet her eyes closed and she drifted into a peaceful, dreamless sleep.

Hours later she awoke, naked and cold on top of the covers next to Olivia who was tightly curled against her. She tried to pull the covers up and over them but quickly realized that wasn't possible. She kissed Olivia on the forehead, the tip of her nose and finally on her lips before she received a response. Within seconds, she forgot about being cold. Their passion left them both gasping for breath, arms wrapped around each other.

"You're cold," Olivia noticed, running her hand up and down Rebecca's arm.

"Yeah, so are you. That's why I was waking you up, to tell you we need to get under the covers."

"You found a very effective way to awaken me," Olivia teased, smiling at Rebecca.

"Let's get under the covers and I'll see if I can wake you up some more," Rebecca suggested.

"Promise?"

"Definitely," Rebecca vowed.

Rebecca quickly discovered some problems with making love under the covers and their efforts shoved the comforter to the floor and twisted the blanket and sheet into a tangled mess. Finally, their desires quenched, Rebecca pulled the tangled mess up over herself and Olivia, keeping them wrapped in a warm cocoon the rest of the night.

CHAPTER NINETEEN

Five Months Later

Memorial Day weekend started out with rain, but by Monday the ground had dried and the sun was shining brightly. Rebecca and her father had spent the previous weekend at Peacock Cemetery with a weedeater and shovels, cleaning up the rundown patch of ground as best they could. They righted overturned stones, straightened markers that were leaning precariously, and shoveled dirt into the old, sunken graves to level the ground, sprinkling new grass seed and straw over the top of the fresh dirt. Rebecca's dad said he had been planning to clean the old cemetery up someday anyway, and their plans for Memorial Day had only provided him the excuse he needed to put it at the top of his "To Do" list. Rebecca was proud of their efforts and had even remembered to bring another hinge for the broken gate.

The past few months had been full of changes in Rebecca's life and she had enjoyed spending the weekend working with her father again. She and Olivia had divided the week after Christmas between Olivia's apartment and Rebecca's parents' house. Olivia had loved the cups she had made her, and wore the silver bracelet nearly every day. Rebecca treasured the heart necklace Olivia had given her.

Since school started back in January, she had spent nearly every other weekend at Olivia's apartment. The few other weekends she had been busy catching up on her homework and planning for the future. She had switched her classes for the upcoming fall semester to the main campus of the community college, closer to St. Louis. She and Olivia had found an apartment to lease halfway between their colleges and each would be driving thirty minutes to classes. Rebecca had been boxing up her possessions for two weeks and they were moving the first of June. After each weekend she had spent with Olivia it had become harder to return home, and she was looking forward to sharing an apartment with her full-time.

Kate had gotten over her animosity and even talked about coming to the city to shop with Olivia sometime. Grandma had surprised them all. Although Rebecca had not explained her relationship with Olivia to her yet, she had asked Rebecca one weekend when she and Olivia were visiting why she didn't marry her young woman before she got away. It was the only time Rebecca had ever seen Olivia blush. After her initial shock passed, Rebecca had responded, "Well, Grandma, you make a good point there. I'll definitely take that under advisement."

That Memorial Day morning she had ridden over to Peacock Cemetery with her parents. They didn't have to wait long before they heard another car proceeding slowly along the gravel road toward them.

When the car pulled up outside the evenly hanging gate that Monday, everyone but Rebecca and her dad was surprised at the transformation of the old cemetery. Olivia hugged Rebecca, then Willie, as she exclaimed over the improvements. Eliza thanked them both as well. Even though her memories of the cemetery were lit by headlights, the changes were obvious.

Rebecca stood near her parents and allowed Olivia, Eliza, and Grandmama to step up to Mary Farthing's grave.

Grandmama had insisted on coming today. She said she had to right a wrong. She wouldn't elaborate and Eliza and Olivia were both puzzled by her request.

Grandmama walked up to MJ's headstone, set her oversize handbag down gently then knelt down in front of it. "I'm sorry, Mother," she said quietly. "I didn't know. You should have told me."

She took a large urn from the bag and set it on the ground in front of the stone. Eliza gasped loudly, but Grandmama appeared not to notice. She said quietly, "I forgive you for not being there for me. Please forgive me for not understanding."

Eliza quickly looked over to Olivia, then Rebecca and her parents and placed a finger to her lips to ensure their silence. Rebecca's parents looked a little puzzled but Olivia smiled and nodded, knowing the truth wouldn't change anything except for incurring Grandmama's wrath upon Eliza and her brothers.

Grandmama stood and walked over to Rebecca's father. "Mr. Wilcox, would you be so kind to help me with something? I desire to inter this urn here over MJ's resting place. Would you be so kind to help me with this matter?"

He could see the pleading look on Eliza's face over her mother's shoulder and he assured her he would bring over a shovel that very afternoon to do her bidding.

Grandmama turned and gestured toward Olivia and Rebecca, calling them to her. As they neared, she held out a hand to each. They stood facing her, nervous and uncertain of her intentions.

"Girls, I need to say something to you, too. I have asked for my mother's forgiveness but now I realize I need to ask for yours as well. I have caused my granddaughter and her lovely friend unnecessary pain. Can you find it in your hearts to forgive a foolish old woman who didn't even try to understand?"

Rebecca nodded mutely, unable to voice the emotions the usually stern, remote woman had evoked in her.

Olivia squeezed Grandmama's hand. "Of course, I'll forgive you, Grandmama. I love you."

"Let us make a vow to not allow hatred, fear or misunder-standing to cause pain to those we love so much, to our family." Grandmama looked around at Eliza, Beth and Willie.

Eliza stepped forward and took Olivia's free hand, then reached for Willie's hand. Beth had taken Rebecca's hand and held her husband's hand as well. The six stood in a small circle in front of the final resting place of Mary and Jane.

Smiling at Olivia then Rebecca, Eliza promised, "My grandmothers' lives may have suffered irreparable damage, but I vow I will do everything in my power to see that the same thing doesn't happen to my daughter or her friends."

"We are always here for you both," Beth declared. Willie solemnly nodded his agreement.

Rebecca ducked her head, embarrassed, but cherishing the love and support. She knew she would need it to make it through the days and years ahead.

Grandmama turned to walk toward the gate but Olivia stopped her. "Grandmama, I want to get a picture of you, Mom and me, in front of MJ's stone. Rebecca, would you use my camera to take a picture, please?"

Rebecca had Olivia kneel on one side of the stone, her mother and grandmother on the other. Rebecca snapped the photo then checked to see if it was a good one.

Turning a little pale as she looked at the images on the camera display, she stammered, "Uh, Olivia, I think you need to see this."

Olivia hurried over and took the camera. She was strangely silent for a few seconds, then, wordlessly walked over to her mother and Grandmama and showed them the picture. Rebecca's parents exchanged wondering looks, quickly changing to looks of concern as Grandmama gasped loudly. Suddenly, Eliza grabbed her mother to keep her standing as her knees buckled beneath her. Grandmama quickly recovered although she was oddly pale.

Rebecca walked over and reached for the camera, saying, "May I?"

Eliza handed it to her and she took it to her parents. "Well, I'll be!" her dad exclaimed. "I guess it *has* been haunted all these years."

Sitting atop the headstone, smiling at the women kneeling beside them, were two foggy images easily recognizable as the two women from the photo Olivia had investigated months before.

Rebecca walked over and took Olivia's hand. "We answered all of our questions," she reminded her.

Olivia didn't answer. Instead they stood silently together and listened to the sound of light laughter slowly drifting away with the wind.